MW01204165

Zuccotti Park

ZUCCOTTI PARK

ANDREW SERRA

TUDOR CITY PRESS

Cover design by Jason Arias

Cover art adapted from photograph by Koshu Kunii / Unsplash

Author photo by Teresa Perretta

ISBN: 978-1-7322380-4-6

Library of Congress Control Number: 2021925349

Tudor City Press

New York, NY

For Luca

1

WEDNESDAY

The sea wind on the ferry was different from other sea winds, Frank thought. He'd never been a fisherman, but imagined something more pure about the salty air aboard a coastal trawler. On the ferry there was diesel exhaust. In the rain you smelled wet shoes and the bathrooms always stank of urine. You could even smell it on the forward deck. Frank had hardly ever ridden the ferry prior to his assignment on the boat. He stared out at the choppy water and wondered if this would be his last ride.

Manhattan had the skyline and Brooklyn had its bridge. Queens had two airports and the Bronx had its ball club. But Staten Island—that plain little island—had a ferry. That's not to say all Staten Islanders rode the ferry. Workday commuters who lived conveniently near the connecting train line took the ferry, and those heading in for Manhattan's nightlife. Many islanders, however, found it an unnecessary or unpleasant means of transportation. Frank saw little reason to ever ride it again.

The sun gave little warmth as the aged vessel cut through the waves. The wind pushed his hair back while he leaned on the railing and watched the island get closer. The familiar air filled his lungs. In his back pocket was a worn leather wallet. Frank stepped back from the railing and took it out, feeling its lightness. Inside there was an empty cutout in the shape of a police badge. On the other fold was a clear window with nothing behind it. From a small Manila envelope he removed a brand new I.D. card. *Retired Police Officer* was stamped below his photo and he slid the card into the window before putting the wallet back in his pocket.

The boat docked hard and the few midday passengers on deck were jolted forward. He stepped onto the ramp as two cops were walking up. The first was a Black man in his mid-forties and the other skinny, white and looking hardly older than a teenager.

"There's my man," the first cop said. "Well how'd it go?"

"I'm officially a civilian," Frank answered plainly.

"Frank—this is my new partner, Tom..."

"Tim!" corrected the young officer.

"Right, Tim."

"I'm Frank," he said, offering a handshake. "Leon's one hell of a cop. Learn all you can from him."

The older cop laughed. "Frank here was your predecessor," he said. "Retired officially o'nine hundred this morning." He leaned back on his heels and rested his hands on the radio holder and ammo pouch of his gun-belt.

Frank looked at the black leather belt—worn and creased and in places faded to brown. He then looked at Tim's—shiny dark and smooth. He remembered being a rookie, scuffing his gun-belt against the locker room wall so the perps wouldn't know he was brand new.

"I'm sorry about your wife," Tim said.

"Thank you," answered Frank with a nod.

Leon motioned up the ramp with his head, "Go on and make sure everyone exits the boat. I'll catch up."

"Ten-four," answered Tim. "It was nice meeting you, Frank."

When the rookie was up the ramp, Leon turned back and waited for a commuter to pass before speaking.

"So how you holding up?"

"I'm fine. I'll be fine, Leon. Really."

"You sure retiring now is a good idea? Last thing you ought to be doing is sitting around the house."

"I'm fine."

"I guess twenty-three years is enough. Another year and a half and I'll be out of here too."

"God help you then, pal. Beverly will send your ass straight to Home Depot!"

Leon laughed. "We'll see about that. She says she wants to sell the place—move down South Carolina. Be near her sister."

"Diane wanted me to retire as soon as I had twenty—but I wanted to wait till Jen was done with school."

"You would've missed me too much," Leon answered, laughing at his own joke with short, baritone guffaws. "That's it!"

"Something like that."

"Got to catch that boat. You and Jen come by next week—Bev would love having you guys over for supper."

"Will do."

"You take care of that little sweetheart!" He patted Frank's shoulder and went up the ramp.

"I wish I knew how," Frank answered, but Leon was already stepping onto the ferry.

2

—·—

F rank sat at the table and drank his beer. It was no longer
cold because he had poured it while cooking and been
too busy following the recipe to drink. The table was small
and twenty years out of style. A small television cluttered the
counter and the news was on.

*"Now entering its second week, protesters say the police have
arrested dozens here for exercising their First Amendment
rights. Police officials won't confirm the exact number of arrests
made here so far, but I can tell you that just a little while ago
on that corner here behind me police arrested two men who
were standing in the street holding placards. There was a bit of
a scuffle before more officers arrived and helped handcuff the
two men. The protesters, however, say they will not be
deterred. As you can see, more tents have been erected around*

the perimeter of the park. Be sure to tune in at eleven for all the latest down here at Zuccotti Park. Back to you Ken."

The reporter stood in front of a police barricade and protesters in the background shouted and waved signs. The picture cut back to the anchor team in studio and Frank sipped his warm beer and thought of the riots in Crown Heights back in 1991. All hell broke loose. Now that was a protest! No one stood neatly behind barricades and waved signs; they torched buildings and killed people. He'd fought for his life in a dark alley using only a nightstick—firing his gun would only have drawn more attackers. These kids here on television whined about Wall Street and said they would fight for justice. They didn't know what it meant to fight.

He heard the front door open and close and then Jen walked into the kitchen. She wore ripped jeans and brown leather work-boots. Her hooded, gray sweatshirt was zipped up to her neck. Her brown hair was tied back in a ponytail. She looked so much like her mother.

"Hey," he said.

"Hey," she whispered and opened the refrigerator. She stood with the door open staring inside.

"I made us some dinner," Frank said.

"Not hungry."

"Then why is the refrigerator open?"

Jen shut the door. Frank looked at his watch and quickly grabbed oven-mitts off the counter and pulled back the oven door. He pulled out a baking dish and set it on the counter. Jen stared in silence.

"It was in the recipe book on the counter—seemed easy enough. So I went to the store and got the ingredients," he announced proudly.

Jen's eyes welled up but she didn't cry. She stormed out of the kitchen and up the stairs.

Frank looked down at the baking dish. Glazed slices of ham sizzled as sweet pineapple and tender roasted-pork aromas wafted above. He felt gut-punched—both angry and breathless. He stared down at the food and took stock of the day. After twenty-three years, he had retired from the Police Department. This was his party—ham for one. He thought of his forty-two-year old wife who'd died of a heart attack just ten days before. His anger turned to suffocating sadness.

Jen stomped heavily down the stairs and went out the front door.

3

"Bud-draught... and back up this sorry mug when he's ready!" shouted someone behind Frank. He had been staring thoughtlessly at the ballgame but now his spell was broken and he turned to see who was there.

"Hey," Frank said.

Even seated on a stool Frank was taller than the man. He had gray hair but was younger than he looked. He wore an Irish tweed cap and he squeezed Frank's shoulder while reaching for his Bud-draught. "How's the pleasure-cruise business?"

"Wouldn't know."

"Don't tell me you went back to being a real cop!"

"Not exactly. Retired this morning."

"Hey, congrats. What are you going to do?"

Frank shrugged his shoulders, took a sip of beer and resumed watching the ballgame.

"Ah. Take a vacation—you and the missus. Don't do nothing for a while," the man added as he too sipped his beer.

Frank nodded without looking away from the T.V.

"I was at One P.P. all day today—kid from the Six-two got jammed-up tuning up some mope on a family dispute. Of course now the mope's wife is sticking up for the scumbag."

"The perks of being a P.B.A. delegate, huh," remarked Frank. "You spend half your time at One Police Plaza with guys who get jammed-up."

"It's not as rewarding as riding the ferry all day! Haha!" The man laughed in a way that annoyed Frank.

"I did fifteen years in the Seven-three asshole!" Frank's answer was sharper than he had intended.

"I'll drink to that!" the man answered, touching his glass to Frank's.

Frank finished his beer and counted the change the bartender had left on the bar. He put few bucks tip under the empty glass and stood to leave.

"I got another one coming for you," said the man and right on cue the bartender placed a full glass in front of Frank. He debated politely refusing. He didn't really feel like talking to the delegate anymore, but the cold frothy pint won out. He sat back on the stool and took a sip.

4

— · —

Jen took the bottle from Jamal's hands and took a swig of beer, then handed it back. They sat on the floor in front of the sofa. The T.V. was on with the volume very low—neither was really watching. She rested her head on his muscular shoulder and caressed his ear.

"Jamal..." she said softly without raising her head.

"Yes."

"Did you tell your mom about me?"

After a moment, he answered in a low voice, "Nah, I don't talk to her about stuff like that."

"Think she'd care that I'm white?"

Jamal paused again before speaking. "It's not *her* reaction I'm worried about."

Jen pulled her head back and looked him in the eye. She rubbed his cheek gently and then leaned in and kissed him. She had never felt such passion before. When they had finished she spoke again.

"I was wrong to tell you not to come to the funeral."

"We just started going out. It's cool."

"I don't care what my father will say. I can go out with whoever I want. If he doesn't like you, he can go to hell." She leaned her head back onto his shoulder and began to cry.

"What's wrong, Baby?" he asked softly.

"It's a long story," she answered between sobs.

Jamal brushed her cheek and kissed the top of her head. He whispered: "It's okay."

Jen took a second and then began speaking.

"A year or two ago, I was sitting at the table doing homework and my mom came home from work with a grocery bag. She just got a new recipe book and she was excited to try it out. She stopped at the store on the way home and bought sliced ham and made the glazing from scratch and put pineapple rings over the top. She baked it in the oven and it was done just as my dad got home. It smelled delicious, but he took one look at it and said 'What the fuck is this?' He wouldn't even try it. So my poor mother, after working all day and having already cooked the bastard dinner once, had to cook him something else."

"Would he have beat her or something?" he interrupted.

"No, nothing like that. But she just wanted to make him happy. She always did. And what does the asshole go ahead and do tonight? He makes glazed sliced ham with pineapple. He doesn't even remember being a prick to my mother over sliced ham. He was a prick whenever she wanted to try something new... or different. But now he wants me to eat the fucking ham and tell him how good it is. Fuck him."

Jamal leaned down and again kissed Jen on top of the head.

"What time's your mom get home?" she asked after sniffling.

"Little after midnight."

"I better get going. Will you walk me down?"

"'Of course," he answered as he turned her chin toward his and kissed her.

She was comforted by his kiss. Talking to Jamal about her father had unburdened her but through her grief arose an all-consuming guilt. "I really am sorry," she whispered when their lips parted.

"For what?" he asked softly.

"The funeral."

5

The crisp air was still and quiet except for the distant roar of a city bus somewhere up Forest Avenue. The newsstand and the clothing boutique had their roll-down gates shut and Frank buried his hands in his pockets as he walked past, regretting having not worn a coat. He turned left on Bement Avenue and passed three blocks of identical, nearly touching, Colonial-style two-story houses. He turned left again and passed two more of the same before climbing the steps of the third. The alcohol and the chilled air on his fingers made getting the key in the door challenging. His head was spinning and he stood up straight and took a deep breath. He was about to try again when he heard a car pulling into the driveway. He turned and saw Diane's red Ford Contour, with its dented front bumper, pulling in and for a split second could swear it was the obscured silhouette of his wife behind the wheel. He stared at the car while Jen shut off the motor and swung the door out.

Jen slammed the car door and climbed the steps. "What are you doing?" she asked.

"My fingers are numb—can't work the lock," said Frank.

Jen's face grimaced with thinly veiled annoyance as the stench of alcohol hit her. Without speaking she opened the door with her own key and went inside.

Jen was halfway up the steps when she heard a crash. She stopped to see what had happened. Frank lay on the floor just inside the doorway. The coat rack was knocked over. Frank stood clumsily and managed to shut the door, then made his way to the armchair in the living room and fell back heavily into the worn cushions.

Jen continued up and then stood still at the top step. With tears running down her cheek she began speaking without turning back. "I remember you and Mommy watching the news once—when I was in second grade. There was something about David Dinkins and you said 'That jig almost ruined this city!' I was standing right here at the top of the stairs—I heard you say that to Mom. I asked my teacher what a jig is and she told me never to say that word again."

She waited for a response but none came. She turned to look down over the railing at her father in the armchair. He began snoring.

6

---·---

THURSDAY

J en parked the red Ford Contour on the gravel along the chain-link fence that separated the college campus from an apartment complex. She was running late and didn't feel like circling for a better spot. The gravel dust made the car dirty but her mother's car was old and beat up anyway so she didn't care. She cut through the faculty lot and followed the walkway past the computer lab in 1N toward the Poli-Sci building—2N. The trees still clung to their auburn foliage while wilted brown leaves blew along the path. The breeze was cool and steady but not strong and the sun shined brightly, high above the cloudless sky. Jen adjusted her backpack and picked up her pace.

"Hey Bitch! Wait for me!" cried a shrill voice from behind.

Jen turned without stopping and smiled. "*Bridge*. We're going to be late again!"

Lagging behind was a tall and skinny young woman with high-blown red hair. Her high-heeled boots made her clumsy strides resemble a fawn's first steps. "Hey, yesterday was *your* fault," she answered as she struggled to keep up with Jen.

The classroom door in the back of the room was propped open so the two sneaked in and sat while Professor Halper was facing the blackboard. Jen scanned the room. The torn-out sheet which students were passing around and signing for attendance was still up front and working its way to the back of the room. She was relieved—if she had missed the sheet she would've had to wait after class and asked the professor to sign it then. She looked around the room. In the row against the far wall, midway back, sat Jamal. He had been waiting to make eye contact with her and he made an exaggerated motion of looking at his watch. They exchanged smiles.

Professor Halper finished writing on the blackboard and then read it aloud:

"Congress shall make no law respecting an establishment of religion, or prohibiting the free exercise thereof; or abridging the freedom of speech, or of the press; or the right of the people peaceably to assemble, and to petition the Government for a redress of grievances."

While the professor was reading Jen rummaged through her backpack for a pen. She pulled one out and tried scribbling in her notebook—no ink! She leaned toward her friend and whispered: "Bridge..."

Bridget stared at the professor without acknowledging Jen. "Bridget!" Jen tried again without breaking the spell.

"What does this mean?" Professor Hapler asked the class and Bridget's hand shot up.

"Ms. Doherty?"

Bridget smiled at the professor and then turned her attention to the blackboard. She twirled a long, curled strand of her fiery red hair with a pen and said: "It's the First Amendment—freedom of speech and stuff."

A couple of students around the room stifled laughs under their breath.

"And *stuff*... yes," answered the professor with a smile.

A hand went up in the front row and the professor pointed to the student with the piece of chalk in his hand while still smiling at Bridget.

"It says the congress shall pass no law, but wouldn't that mean that a state legislature or city council could ban the freedom of speech?" asked the young man.

"As written, yes. But the Fourteenth Amendment bound the states to guarantee the same rights to its citizens." The professor looked around the room, no other hands were up. A silence fell over the room and Jen thought about raising her hand. She hated seeing professors disappointed. It was not that she particularly cared about Halper's approval, she just didn't like *any* professor thinking her generation was uninterested in the state of the world. She tried to think of something smart to ask and though she had strong feelings about the First Amendment, nothing came to mind.

It was instead the professor who broke the silence. "How about Occupy Wall Street? Would we say they were peaceably assembled to redress their grievances?"

Jen waved her hand in the air, as did a few other students..

Professor Halper looked toward Bridget but her hand was not raised. He pointed to Jamal.

"I would say absolutely," the young man answered.

"But there have been numerous scuffles with police, Mr. Barrow. Can we call that peaceful?"

"The protestors arrived with the sole purpose of voicing their opinion. They did not attack a government building or roam the streets terrorizing people. The fights with the cops are because the cops are trying to make the protestors go home." Jamal spoke with zeal and when finished he looked to Jen. She smiled.

"So you would say it was the government—specifically the cops—who are the aggressors. They act outside of the Constitution?"

"Yeah, I guess," said Jamal.

"Anyone else?" asked the professor.

"But if protestors shut down lower Manhattan, a lot of people can't go to work," said a young woman from the back of the room. "Isn't that why we have police—to make sure a few people don't disrupt the lives of the rest of us?"

"So you would argue that the government has a duty to keep the peace?" Halper asked. The student nodded affirmatively. He continued: "Should the government have stopped Martin Luther King from speaking at the March on Washington? After all, the crowd did cause quite a large traffic jam."

"That's different," answered the young woman.

"Why?"

"Because Martin Luther King was protesting racism and brutality. Occupy Wall Street is protesting high credit card rates. It's not the same thing."

"So you object to the content of their grievances?"

"But if large banks can cause an economic meltdown," said Jamal, "doesn't that also affect all of our freedom?"

"I would say yes," answered the professor. "But should the government decide which protests are important and which aren't?"

Jen raised her hand.

"How could we trust the government to make that decision?" she said. "I mean, wouldn't it be in their interest to suppress protests critical of the government?"

Professor Halper nodded in contemplation. "Are there limits? Should the mayor and the police sit back and let waves of protestors shut down highways and bridges whenever they want? Or should there be a balance between a people's right to redress grievances and the government's duty to maintain peace?" He looked around the room, locked eyes with Bridget and spoke. "But what is a right, exactly? Once fought for and won does that right not become a duty? Aren't the people's rights—to be informed, to speak out, to vote—now a sacred duty? Even if it means going to jail! Rights are like muscles. If they are not exercised, they atrophy."

Jamal, Jen, and Bridget followed the pathway leading from 2N toward the cafeteria.

"Shit!" said Bridget as she swung her backpack around to the front. The nylon was frayed around the zipper and the lettering of the College of Staten Island seal was peeling off. "I left my phone. I'll meet you guys over there." She turned and jogged off awkwardly toward 2N in her high-heels. Jamal and Jen continued without her.

The tall glass dome of 1C reflected the autumn sun. Outside the cafeteria entrance, along a curved brick wall stood a table and a small crowd. As the two approached they could read the placards—*We are the 99%!* and *Where's Our Bailout?*

A short young woman with glasses and a pink, hooded College of Staten Island sweatshirt was holding a clipboard and speaking loudly to the crowd. "Join us, six a.m. tomorrow morning—outside the athletic center. We're taking the six-fifteen bus to the ferry and then walking to Zuccotti Park. Let's stand up and fight for justice—six a.m. tomorrow! Who's with us?"

"Want to go?" asked Jen as she leaned into Jamal and wrapped both her hands around his arm.

He shook his head.

"What do you mean, no? What about what you said back there in class—about the protestors standing up for their rights?"

"I do believe they got a right to protest. That don't mean I got to be there with them. Besides, don't you got a class tomorrow morning?"

"Who cares? This is more important. I *do* got to be there! Those bastards scammed billions from our economy and then when they blew everything up—the government bailed them out. We're in school now. What's going to happen in a couple of years when we graduate and have student loans to pay off and we can't find a job? What then?"

"Maybe I'll be stuck with a college degree, a huge debt, and no job," Jamal answered. "But one thing is certain. If I get locked up—I *definitely* won't get a job. You think a Black man with a criminal record has a shot in a job interview? You think the police will hire me if I got a criminal record? These protestors have a lot of great ideas, but sooner or later they'll be tired of protesting and go home—and I'd just be left with a rap sheet."

Jen stood silently, not sure how to respond.

Jamal smiled. "Come on, I'm hungry."

7

Jamal heard Jen's phone buzzing atop the nightstand. She reached an arm out from under the sheet to see who was calling and placed the phone back down without answering. He wrapped his arm around her and kissed her bare shoulder. She was facing away from him as he spooned his naked body up against hers.

"You're not my first," she said softly without turning her head.

Jamal chuckled and kissed her shoulder again. "You're not mine either."

"It was a guy I went to high school with. I didn't love him. And I'm not saying I know how exactly I feel about you now —but I've never felt like this with anyone."

He froze. Jen's words hung awkwardly on the air. It would have been pandering to repeat what she said and, besides, it was too soon to tell her he loved her. He searched his mind frantically—imagining the seconds ticking down on an arena shot clock—and found an acceptable answer just before the buzzer. "I really like you. I've never gone out with someone like you."

"You mean white."

He laughed. "Well, yeah. But that's not what I mean."

"So what do you mean?"

"I mean I never been with a girl who wants to change the world like you do."

"There were no girls in your class who cared about politics?"

"A few. But I ain't been with none of them. The only girls I ever messed around with were the ones here on the block. Guess I figured it was easier to keep things cool—not get too serious."

"Can I ask you something?" she asked, turning her head to look at him.

"Shoot."

"What made you want to be a cop?"

Jamal was quiet for a moment and gently traced a finger across the top of her breasts, caressing her youthful skin. "When I was a kid, the police showed up and arrested my brother Randy. We were playing basketball downstairs and they hopped out of a van and jumped on top of him. He didn't do anything wrong—so he fought back. The cops handcuffed me just so I couldn't help him and after they put Randy in the van, they uncuffed me and drove away. There I was—just a kid—crying on the court because the police dragged my brother off."

"What happened to him?"

"Turns out they had the wrong guy. They was looking for some dude who robbed the bodega with a gun. They dropped the robbery charges but still charged him with resisting arrest."

"That's terrible. I'm sorry."

"I never forgot that—the way I felt standing alone in the basketball court seeing that van take my brother away. I don't ever want another kid to feel that way. That's why I want to be a cop."

"See," said Jen.

"What?"

"You want to change the world too!"

Jamal smiled. "I guess—but I don't get to change anything if I got a criminal record."

Her eyes became sad. "I understand how you feel," she said in a soft tone.

Jamal was about to say something but stopped. His mother was in his head. *I understand how you feel.* Those were the exact words a white coworker had said to his mom after police shot a Black teenager in Brooklyn. Even Jen's tone bothered him. Did she feel sorry for him? He sat up and grabbed his pants off the floor. "I'm not going with you tomorrow," he answered briskly as he slid his jeans up his legs.

Jen sat up and gathered her clothes, but Jamal buttoned his pants without making eye contact.

8

—·—

F rank sat in the living room armchair and flipped through the channels. He had just watched three *Law and Order* episodes in a row and didn't want to get sucked into the next one. Nothing else looked interesting. He checked the time, 11:58. Two beer cans sat on the end table and Frank couldn't remember which he had been drinking. The first one he tried was empty, but a last sip swished around the other when he raised it and Frank downed it. He shut the T.V. off and the room went dark. The street was quiet out front until he heard a car pulling into the driveway. The headlights shone through the living room windows and then went dark and the motor was silent. He heard keys jingle and the door swung in.

"Why didn't you answer your phone?" he said before Jen was even fully in the house.

"I didn't hear it ring. Bridge and I were listening to music and I only noticed I had a missed call when I was leaving."

"You said you'd only use your mother's car to go to school and back. This is two nights in a row you took it out."

She rolled her eyes. "What's the big deal? It was parked outside Bridget's house. It's not like I was out drag racing."

Frank's bottom lip jetted out in an exaggerated frown and he nodded his head up and down. He couldn't think of anything to say.

"I won't use the car anymore," Jen said. She went toward the stairs and started to climb.

"Why are you so angry with me?" he said softly.

Jen stopped on the third step and looked at her father. She had never seen him vulnerable before. Of course he cried at the hospital and at the funeral, but grief and vulnerability are two separate things entirely. Now, sitting in his armchair in the dark room—he looked pathetic. "I'm not angry," she answered plainly and went up to her bedroom. She took out her phone, opened a text message chain with Jamal and started typing: *Are u upset with me?*

Her fingers shook as she typed and her eyes were watery. When she finished, she reread the text and then stared at it for a long while. She deleted the message and put her phone down.

9

FRIDAY

T he iPhone on the end table vibrated and blasted Wagner's *Flight of the Valkyries*. Professor Halper reached an arm up and silenced it without unburying his head from the pillow. He lay motionless for some time before feeling around for his glasses. He sat up and reached for a cigarette. With his thumb he flicked a broken plastic lighter and inhaled deeply, then leaned his head back against the headboard. There were dirty clothes all across the floor. His bedspread was completely twisted around the sheet—the bed had not been made in quite some time.

In his late thirties and never married, he had only known love unhappily. Five years had been spent on and off with a colleague who would never leave her husband. For the past three years he was alone and had given up on love entirely, until the first day of class that semester. That was when he first saw her. The weather was still warm and she came in the classroom laughing with another student. She wore short denim shorts and her long legs were perfectly outlined with lean and muscular thighs. The complexion of her skin—a tanned-pale whiteness—betrayed both her Irish heritage and a summer spent at the beach. She had a loose tank top on and though her breasts were not large, the bra she wore pushed up some cleavage above the baggy neckline. Then there was her hair, that amazing red hair painted by the gods to personify the fire lit in his soul. He was once again alive.

He felt no guilt over his feelings. There wasn't a professor alive who has never been attracted to a student before, he thought. The only difference was that he finally had the balls to do something about it. What could happen? He'd lose his job. So what? He spent years working on his doctorate while teaching as an adjunct. Being an adjunct was insulting— teaching students and earning less than the janitors out in the hall. It's like those barber schools that make you cut the hair of paying customers while you wait for them to give you a diploma. The university didn't charge students less tuition for taking classes taught by adjuncts, they just pocketed the difference. And now what? He had his PhD, but instead of a full associate professor position he was offered just four sections of undergrad Poli-Sci at the College of Staten Island— still little more than an adjunct, just a slightly higher pay scale.

He got out of bed and smashed his cigarette out in an ashtray on the end table. At his feet were a flannel shirt and a pair of jeans and he picked them up and smelled them. Good enough. The bohemian look seemed to work for Bridget, but of course it's always difficult to know for sure with these kids. She may have just been flirting to court a higher grade or leeway with a term paper. She *did* come to his office yesterday. He'd expected it after seeing her cellphone was left on the desk. It could not have been an accident. He shared an office with two other professors but both were in class. He shut the door so she would have to knock. Sure enough a minute later there was a light tap on the door.

"Professor..." she said timidly as she peeked her head around the door. She then entered and shut the door behind her. His plan had worked.

"I think I left my phone in class."

"I have it here," he answered and stepped closer to hand it over.

She took it in both hands as if receiving a communion wafer and looked up at him coyishly. Later that night he would reproach himself for not kissing her right there. It seemed so clear in hindsight, she would have gone for it. But he hesitated and to fill the moment she spoke.

"I liked your lecture today."

"Thanks," he answered while looking her in the eye. "Do you really care about Occupy Wall Street?"

She nodded. "I think it's the defining moment of our generation, like when the students protested Vietnam."

He had a bold thought. "Do you want to go there with me?"

She smiled and blushed. "When?"

"Tomorrow morning."

"Okay." She looked down at her hands and started pushing buttons on her iPhone. "What's your number?"

He told her without hesitation and a second later *Flight of the Valkyries* was blasting from his pocket. He looked at the screen, "That's you?"

"Yep. Text me later and let me know what time. I'll meet you at the ferry terminal." She touched her hand to his forearm and turned and went out. His heart beat like a marching band drum.

As the door shut he heard her high-heels clopping down the hall and he took his glasses off and wiped his forehead on his sleeve. His phone let out a loud ding. Text message. It was from the same phone number—but the message was just a symbol and a number, side by side: <3. He knew enough about text message slang to feel a sharp rise of sexual excitement rush through his body.

Halper thought about that text message as he shuffled through his bedroom closet to find a sleeping bag and a two-person bivouac tent zipped into a pouch. He stuffed both into a backpack. He grabbed a fleece pullover off the bed and put his cigarettes into an outer pocket of the backpack. He slid his wallet and keys into his jeans pockets and left the apartment.

10

—·—

Jen sat alone on the ferry. Her College of Staten Island backpack was on her lap. A group of C.S.I. students were all clumped together at the front of the boat wearing varying degrees of school paraphernalia. She hadn't met them at the athletic facility. There was little sense in taking a bus to C.S.I. only to then take another bus back the way she'd come. She just walked to Forest Avenue from her house and took a bus straight to the ferry terminal. She didn't feel like sitting with them now anyway—preferring to stare out the window.

It was a newer boat with plenty of stainless steel. The announcements were both louder and more audible. The counter that served coffee and pretzels and beer had glass sneeze guards instead of how the old boats kept an open pretzel tree on a stained Formica counter. Weekday morning ferries were usually filled with nothing but commuters, but there was still the occasional tourist and a French couple snapped pictures of the Statue of Liberty as the crowded boat pushed itself past the lady of the harbor.

"Well-well-well... Hello there, young lady."

Jen turned to see Leon, police cap tilted high on his head, sipping a cup of coffee. She immediately stood, left the backpack on her seat, and went over and hugged him. The crowd of commuters read their papers and texted on their phones and paid little attention to the young woman hugging a uniformed cop in front of them.

"How you holding up there, Missy?"

"I'm good. How's Bev?"

"She good, she good. Where you off to?"

"Museum. School project." Jen wasn't sure why she lied.

"That's my girl. You stay in those books now."

She nodded and smiled.

"How's Pop doing?"

Jen paused for the quickest of seconds and gave the stock answer, "Good, he's good."

"I worry about him. He's not just sitting around the house, is he?"

Jen shrugged her shoulders and looked out the window at the Jersey City harbor in the distance.

"I know he don't always know how to say it—but he loves you very much." Leon gently put his hands on Jen's shoulders and spun her to face him.

Jen nodded her head silently—fearing tears would follow words.

"What museum you going to?"

"MOMA," she answered quickly.

"Well, have fun. I told your Pop, Bev would love having you two over for supper real soon," Leon said with a melancholic smile.

"That sounds nice."

She was surprised by a sight in the background behind Leon. Along the opposite row of windows sat Professor Halper and Bridget. They were sitting awfully close and leaning into each other to speak. Jen returned her gaze to Leon. He smiled, rubbed her shoulder kindly and walked away.

Jen hurriedly sat and rifled through her backpack pockets. She needed to text Bridget. She needed to know what the hell was going on. She checked every pocket of the backpack before a nervous queasiness erupted in the pit of her stomach. The phone was not there, and she instantly remembered putting it in her jacket pocket before opting at the last moment to wear a zip-up sweatshirt instead. What a dumbass! she thought, feeling completely naked without her phone.

11

Frank nestled under the covers as the cool air from an open window chilled the room. His mouth was dry and his temples and forehead throbbed. It hurt to open his eyes; he had to piss so badly his abdomen hurt. He wanted nothing more than to stay under the blanket, but he would wet the bed if he didn't get up. He went to the bathroom and peed through three minutes of head-pounding torture. Returning to his bedroom he heard the loud ding of an iPhone message come from Jen's room. Her door was closed. Wasn't it a bit early for texts? There was no ambition today but sleeping—being awake was too depressing.

12
-·-

The ferry docked and at a slight distance Jen followed Bridget and Halper down the ramp and out to the street. They walked up Broadway, past the charging bronze bull, and continued up toward Zuccotti Park. Hundreds of people were walking the same route. Many were clearly protestors coming to join the movement, the rest were just trying to get to work. She lost sight of them passing Trinity Church as the sidewalk became more and more crowded. At the corner of Broadway and Cedar Street the space in front of her opened up to reveal a spacious square. It was not yet eight o'clock but the park was teaming with activity. Whistles blew and drums beat rhythmically while repetitive chants could be heard but not deciphered. Jen stopped at the corner and took in the scene. An army of cops surrounded the park, which was corralled by police barriers. From symmetrical rows of trees, leafed tree limbs hovered over the protesters, juxtaposed oddly by the massive One Liberty Plaza skyscraper looming behind. In the foreground stood a bright red mass of steel I-beams welded to form interlocking, inverted pyramids. It was called the *Joie de Vivre* and its brightness gave it a lighthouse-type quality, beaconing the passing protestors to this island of social consciousness.

"Zuccotti Park!" she whispered to herself in awe at how small it looked compared to the size of the attention the park had been getting. It did not seem possible that hundreds of protestors, with tents, could fit in the penned-in area.

Jen crossed the street and followed the police barrier around the semicircular eastern border to the park entrance and descended a small set of steps. She made eye contact with everyone she passed and each nodded and smiled. Only the people along the barriers were really holding up signs and chanting, further inside the park people spoke in groups or stood aside and fiddled with their phones. Looking around at the scene, Jen nearly tripped over a woman kneeling.

"Sorry," said Jen.

"No problem," answered the woman without standing. She was a thin, white woman in her mid forties. From a backpack, she handed out granola bars and juice boxes to two children beside her—a boy of ten, perhaps, and a girl slightly younger.

Jen stepped around them and worked her way toward the center of the park, through clusters of tents. She saw a stone bench and sat, swinging her backpack off her shoulder and holding it on her lap. She looked around for Bridget and Halper but couldn't find them.

13

Through the pillow over his head and the closed door, Frank heard the sudden chorus of Maroon 5's *Moves Like Jagger* issuing faintly down the hall. He knew it was *Moves Like Jagger* because he liked Maroon 5 and he knew it was coming from Jen's cellphone. Adam Levine sang to a low-pitched, tinny, iPhone version of the song for about twenty seconds before it stopped. He looked over at the clock: quarter after eight. Who the hell was calling her this early? It wasn't Bridget, he thought, her ring tone was *Last Friday Night* by Katy Perry. And it didn't sound like Jen answered. If she had gone downstairs or even to the bathroom she would have taken her phone. He was now curious and he stood and went down the hall to her room and knocked. There was no answer and he opened the door. Jen wasn't there, but at that moment a message alert rang from the direction of a jacket flung on the bed.

Frank picked up the jacket and found the phone. The screen showed a text message, a missed call, and a voicemail. He slid the bar at the bottom of the screen to open it, but the passcode keyboard opened and he felt guilty for having even slid the bar. He put the phone down on the bed and went downstairs. There was no sign of her there either. He couldn't remember if she had an early class that morning. He looked out the window—Diane's car was in the driveway. He made a pot of coffee and turned on the T.V. The news program was live from Zuccotti Park as the reporter covered the day's Occupy Wall Street developments. It seemed to be the largest crowd gathered there yet.

"*Yesterday's announcement by Police Commissioner Kelly that the Police Department would not force protesters to leave what is essentially a private park—unless the owners requested such a move—seems to have emboldened the demonstrators as today's crowd is the largest yet. I am being told that later today protesters plan to march on Police Headquarters to protest what they call instances of police brutality, including last week's spraying of a group of protestors with pepper spray by a deputy-chief. The incident was caught on tape and has caused widespread outrage among opponents of the police department's actions here so far.*"

Frank shook his head in disgust and walked away from the T.V. He'd like to see one of those liberal fucks try to control an angry crowd, he thought as he reached into the cupboard for a coffee mug. Just then he heard another round of *Moves Like Jagger* playing from Jen's phone upstairs. He now stomped angrily up the steps and retrieved the phone. It was still ringing. Jamal was the name of the caller and he just stared at it and let it go to voicemail again.

Who the hell was Jamal? And then the next thought appeared: sounds Black. He had spent fifteen years in Brownsville and he knew a Black name when he saw one. No Italian or Irish people named their kids Jamal. Who is he and why is he calling Jen?

Frank again opened the passcode keyboard on the screen and typed in 0709, Jen's birthday. WRONG PASSCODE—TRY AGAIN. He thought for a moment and then hit 0311, Diane's birthday. Open. He opened the received text message. It was from Jamal: *Sorry about last nite, call me.* He went to the contacts and looked up Jamal, no last name and a 917 area code —could be from anywhere in the city. He then went to Bridget's contact info and clicked on her number. It rang several times and then Bridget picked up.

"Hey Bitch, what're you doing up this early?" she answered. There was shouting in the background as Bridget yelled into the phone.

"Bridget, it's Frank. I'm looking for Jen."

"Oh shit! Sorry Mr. Scala. She's not with me."

"When was the last time you saw her?"

"Yesterday at school. Why? Is everything okay?"

"I'm sure everything's fine. Tell her to call me if you see her. All right?"

"Sure, Mr. Scala. No problem."

"Thanks," he added as he ended the call. Why had Jen lied to him? She had claimed to be with Bridget the night before and clearly she was with this Jamal. He was not yet alarmed at her disappearance. Of course she'd turn up, but he needed to get to the bottom of this.

14

—·—

"Everything all right?" Halper asked Bridget as she hung up the phone. He was jostled to and fro by the shouting protesters who crowded him against the police barrier railing.

"That was my friend's dad. He's just wondering if I'd seen her." The crowd pushed up behind Bridget and she was pressed forward against his chest. "I hope everything's all right," she added.

"You talking about Jennifer Scala?"

"Yeah."

"She's right there."

Bridget turned to look in the direction Halper had indicated. Twenty feet or so back from the crowd sat Jen on a stone bench. She wrapped a hairband around her fingers and reached behind her head to fix her hair in a ponytail. She sat with her backpack on her lap and seemed to be taking in the whole scene.

15

—·—

F rank drove his gray GMC pick-up down Richmond Terrace toward the northern tip of Staten Island. The tree-lined promenade, with its nineteenth-century mansions up on the hill overlooking the terrace, was a fossil of a bygone era, when horse drawn buggies trotted their well-to-do passengers along the picturesque waterfront. Now, Richmond Terrace overlooked a shoreline full of half-sunk abandoned barges and partially submerged car tires. The mansions on the hill shared their view of the harbor with the housing projects built just below them and the well-to-do drove automobiles over the Verrazano Bridge and never saw Richmond Terrace.

The Staten Island Ferry terminal sat at the corner where Richmond Terrace became Bay Street, opposite Borough Hall and the courthouse. Next to the ferry terminal was the Staten Island Yankees' minor-league baseball stadium, the project which embodied the hopes of politicians for a revitalization of the north shore. A decade later, however, most of those hopes had fizzled out like so many of the Class A ballplayers who had passed through the stadium's gates.

Frank slowed until he saw an empty parking space. It was always a bitch to find parking there, but he was in luck. It was an *Official Parking Only* spot and he pulled down his sun visor to grab his police parking placard. He looked at it for a second, *2011*—his last one. He wouldn't get one next year. He put it up on the dashboard and got out.

On the south side of Richmond Terrace, directly across from the ballpark was the 120th Police Precinct. Well over a hundred years old, the precinct house was falling apart. Construction scaffolding had been erected on the front about ten years before and had never been taken down, despite the fact that no construction was presently being done. He had been assigned to the Staten Island Ferry Detail, but they used to turn out of the 120th Precinct house, so Frank knew most of the cops who worked there.

He walked up the steps and in the front door. The cop at the small desk just inside the doorway knew him and only gave a head nod as Frank went by. He passed by the tall, worn-wooden desk where a sergeant was talking and writing at the same time and went down the hallway to an open door. He looked in the small, disheveled office but there was no one there. He reached in his pocket and took out a fold of paper. *Jamal Barrow* was written on it.

Jen must have emptied her backpack and taken it with her. Her textbooks were on her desk along with a five-subject spiral notebook. Frank had flipped through the pages looking for her class schedule to see if she was supposed to be at class but instead he found a photocopy of a torn-out loose-leaf page. It was a list of email addresses for the students of POL 103, all hand written—the type some eager classmate passes around the first day of class and then photocopies for everyone else. One of the email addresses began *jamal.barrow1115*. It had to be *the* Jamal.

A cop in plain-clothes with a badge hanging on a chain around his neck returned to the office.

"Hey there! I heard you retired. Congratulations brother!" He was white, with salt and pepper hair, mid-forties and he shook Frank's hand warmly. "How you holding up? Since your wife..."

Frank shook his head up and down reflexively and answered without thinking: "I'm good... I'm good."

"You need anything, just let me know."

"Yeah Smitty, I kind of need a favor," he said in a hushed voice.

Smitty looked up and down the hallway and answered quietly, "Shoot!"

"Can you run this name for me?" he asked as he held out the paper.

Smitty shrugged his shoulders and grimaced. "They really monitor this stuff now."

After a second, he added, "Tell you what. When the P.A.A. goes on meal..." he looked at his watch, "in about ten minutes, I'll use the computer in the One-two-four Room."

"Thanks."

"I'll come around the corner and meet you at the coffee shop."

16

— · —

Jen and Bridget sat on the ground with their legs crossed in front. They were in the front row of a crowd gathered around a stone bench. On the bench stood a tall skinny man in his early thirties. His flannel shirt was untucked and he wore a red nylon camping vest over it. He had a week-old beard and yelled his speech—in ten second bursts—pausing to let others fifty feet back or so repeat his message. City law prohibited the use of loudspeakers without a permit, hence this medieval town crier-like system had been revived.

"Right now... At this very moment, the banks and Wall Street firms are pouring millions of dollars into defeating *Dodd-Frank*..." he stopped and waited for the repeaters to shout it forward. "They are pouring millions of dollars into watering down the *C.F.P.B.*..." He paused again. "They ask for billions in bailouts and then they use *our* money to lobby against our own protections!"

A few in the front row clapped before realizing they should wait. After the message had been repeated, a large cheer and a round of applause went through the crowd. Wading through the crowd came Halper. He snaked his body through the throng of standing listeners in the periphery before stepping over the tightly-packed seated protestors up front. Bridget moved closer to Jen and he sat beside her. He took two water bottles out of his pocket and handed one to Jen. The other he opened and sipped from before offering it to Bridget. Jen tilted her head back and drank, while watching the awkward sight of the other two sharing water. The speaker went on shouting his diatribe and Halper addressed Bridget and Jen.

"Michael Moore spoke here two nights ago."

"That's so awesome," said Bridget. "Do you think anyone else famous will show up today?"

"I wouldn't be surprised," he answered.

Jen said nothing as she looked up to the speaker on the bench. The crowd clapped and cheered again and she had no idea what he had just said.

"They're marching to Police Headquarters today. Should we go?" asked Halper.

"What for?" asked Bridget.

"To protest the police chief who pepper sprayed that girl the other day—and all the other instances of brutality so far."

"You in, Jen?" Bridget asked.

Jen still stared up at the man yelling from the bench and Bridget shook her arm. "JEN."

Jen's trance was broken. "Huh?"

"You want to march to Police Headquarters?"

"No. I'll wait here," she answered politely.

"What about standing up for what's right?" asked Halper.

A shot of fury blasted through Jen's veins. Was he for real? Was it right to hang all over a student twenty years younger than you? Who the fuck was he? But she checked her anger and answered calmly. "I don't want any run-ins with the cops today."

"Her dad's a cop," added Bridget.

"Retired!" Jen corrected before returning her gaze to the standing speaker.

"Look, no one has anything against the cop on the beat. It's the policies of the bigwigs we're against. No one's going there to attack the cops," said Halper.

Jen didn't respond or even turn her head toward him. Undeterred, he began speaking to Bridget about the repeal of Glass-Steagall. Bridget listened intently.

Jen just looked up at the speaker on the bench.

17

Frank sat in his armchair thinking. The television was off and he sat in the quiet living room holding a sheet of paper in one hand and Jen's phone in the other. He hit the home button again and read the text from Bridget's phone: *Dad, its me. just met up with Bridge. staying at her place 2nite. c u 2moro.* Again he tried calling Bridget's phone—straight to voicemail. She must have either turned off her phone or was muting his calls. He'd never liked that Bridget, he thought. But then it was probably Jen telling her not to answer.

He looked at the sheet of paper. In Smitty's handwriting were two names: *Jamal C. Barrow, DOB 07/11/61, 2526 3 AVE #3C, Bronx, NY;* and *Jamal L. Barrow, DOB 11/15/91, 315 Grandview Avenue #5B, Staten Island, NY.* He knew the latter was the guy. He knew the address well.

The N.Y.P.D.'s Staten Island Ferry Detail shared a radio frequency with the 120th Precinct. 315 Grandview Avenue was part of the Mariners Harbor Housing Project and he had heard the address read out over the air many times. That project complex had one of the highest crime rates on Staten Island—notorious for gang violence and drug wars. He brooded over the address. What the hell was she doing with this guy?

It wasn't the skin color that bothered him. That would be racist. It was the fact that he was from the projects. He knew the projects well, after all. He had spent fifteen years in Brownsville, Brooklyn's 73rd Precinct—a neighborhood with perhaps the largest concentration of housing projects in the country. He closed his eyes and remembered the last tour he had worked in the Seven-three.

It was a cold winter night, well after midnight, and Frank was almost sweating in the patrol car. His partner, Ray, had the heat blasting and Frank felt his bulletproof vest sticking to his back underneath his turtleneck shirt and coat. Ray was driving slowly down Rockaway Avenue with the headlights off and stopping before the intersection of each corner to see what was going on down the block before the police car was spotted. There were no other cars on the road, but a young child rode a bicycle on the sidewalk—his hooded sweatshirt zipped up tight, no winter coat. In front of the bodega at the corner of

Livonia Avenue, a group of young men laughed loudly as a train rumbled overhead on the elevated tracks.

"Guess no one has to be up early for work tomorrow!" Ray commented to Frank as they passed the group on the corner.

Frank laughed.

Though they'd surely noticed the patrol car passing, none of the group made any visible acknowledgment. Frank had his police radio removed from his belt and it was wedged in the door handle. A two-second digital tone caught his attention. Dispatchers used the tone to precede a priority call. Frank grabbed the radio and held it closer to his ear. Ray reached to his belt and made his own radio louder. A monotone woman's voice read off the job:

"Attention units... In the confines of the Seven-three... announcing a Ten-thirty-four... Assault in progress with a weapon in front of Two-six-seven Livonia Avenue. Female caller states Male-Black wearing a black, puffy coat with a gun at that location."

Ray immediately swung the patrol car into a U-turn. The job was right around the corner. Frank put the radio to his mouth.

"Three-David responding," he said in matter-of-fact tone.

"Housing-Post Nine responding," a man's voice called over the air.

"Three-Adam respo..." a woman added quickly before being stepped on by another man's voice.

"Three-Crime-One responding."

The car swerved around quickly and one tire went up on the sidewalk. The group of young men standing on the corner jumped aside although the car hadn't really come that close to them. They began yelling taunts at the cops as the tire fell off the curb and Ray straightened out the wheels.

"That's all I need is to run over a couple of *Canadians* with an R.M.P.!" said Ray as he kept his eyes on the road and punched the accelerator. The headlights were still off and neither Ray nor Frank switched on the overhead strobes or siren; they were but a few hundred feet from the location of the call and didn't want to give warning to any possible gunman.

Frank gave a quick glance to the men shouting taunts as they sped away from them. They were all Brownsville natives, of course, but *Canadian* was cop-talk for African-American. Twenty years prior, two white cops in an R.M.P., or patrol car, would have had no qualms about calling them n——. But times had changed and it was now a bad career move to be overheard using such language.

They turned onto Livonia Avenue and halfway down the block a tall, Black man (or perhaps even teen-ager), wearing a hooded, black puffy coat stood pointing a gun at another man lying in the street. There had not yet been any sound of gunfire. A small crowd stood behind parked cars on the sidewalk pointing toward the gunman. Ray accelerated and then screeched to a stop, mid-block, thirty feet or so ahead of him. Both car-doors swung out and Ray and Frank both drew their guns and crouched behind their respective doors for cover.

"Drop it!" shouted both cops in unison.

In an instant—before either could react—the gunman spun toward the car and Frank heard three loud pops. The loud cracks echoed off the iron L-train stanchions. Before the last pop rang out, Frank was squeezing his trigger—not knowing how many times he pulled it. The gunman ran off down the block and Frank got back in the car and pulled his door closed shouting, "Go, go, go!" to Ray.

Frank kept his eyes on the gunman. Ray did not get back inside the car. Frank looked over to see his partner's slumped body—half in the car, half out—not moving.

Multiple sirens now wailed loudly and other police cars screeched to a halt from all directions. Frank yanked his radio from his belt but before he could speak, a voice shouted over the air:

"Ten-thirteen... Ten-thirteen... Officer shot!"

Frank sat in his armchair and stared at the sheet of paper with Jamal's name and address. No warrants, he thought. That's one good thing at least. He then looked over to the framed citation on the wall: *The New York City Police Department Combat Cross*. Ray took a bullet to the head and died instantly and Frank was awarded the Combat Cross for wounding the gunman, who was soon captured. The police commissioner himself came to the scene of the shooting and later on, after the funeral, when the commissioner gave Frank the obligatory, "Let me know if there's anything I can do for you!"—Frank asked for a transfer to the Staten Island Ferry Detail.

He stood and went up the stairs to his bedroom. In his nightstand drawer was a copy of his police shield, or dupe. It looked just like the real thing. Officially prohibited, most cops had dupes made to carry around off-duty, so as not to lose their official shield (no cop called it a badge). He traced his finger over the numbers: first the two, then the five, then the seven, and finally the eight. For twenty-three years he had worn that number, *2578*. He looked at the numbers and laughed quietly as he thought about how many times he had played it in the Pick-4, never winning. In the drawer also was a black leather badge holder with a beaded metallic neck chain. He fastened the shield to the holder and put it around his neck, tucking it in his shirt. He then took a holstered gun out of the drawer. It was his off-duty gun—a silver-colored, snub-nosed, five-shot revolver. It was in a scuffed and faded leather "pancake" holster. He unbuckled his belt and passed it through the belt-loops of the holster. From his closet, he took out a button-down flannel shirt and put it on, making sure to cover the gun with the untucked tail of the shirt.

18

—·—

J en sat on the stone bench and ate an apple. It was now after lunchtime and the park was less crowded than it had been in the morning. Many of the protestors had marched to Police Headquarters, including Bridget and Halper. Jen chomped through the shiny Red Delicious and sipped the tea she had bought at the deli across the street after she went in to use the bathroom. Along the barrier, she noticed a man—late thirties with a wool hat and granny glasses—carrying a young girl on his shoulders. The girl held up a cardboard sign but Jen couldn't see the writing. The man bounced with the rhythm of the incessant drumbeat and chanting protestors and whenever he turned his body to the left, Jen could she the girl's face. She was smiling radiantly and chanting with the crowd:

"They got bailed out..."

[Drumbeat] *Boom-Boom... Boom-Boom-Boom!*

"We got sold out!"

[Drumbeat] *Boom-Boom... BOOM-BOOM!*

Jen watched the young girl enjoying the moment and thought of a day some years before when she was twelve. The 120th Precinct (along with the Staten Island Ferry Detail) had organized a trip to Six Flags Great Adventure. A yellow school bus was hired and many of the off-duty cops brought their sons, daughters, nieces, or nephews. Leon brought Bev's niece Jacqueline and Frank brought Jen. They laughed the whole way down the New Jersey Turnpike at Leon's impersonations. At the park they went on all of the rides—even the tall roller coasters—and ate cotton candy and saw the Beach Boys perform a concert at the outdoor stage in the park. They were far from the stage and Frank lifted Jen up onto his shoulders to see. He bopped and swayed to *Help me, Rhonda* and sang in an exaggeratedly deep voice and Jen laughed and sang too. On the bus ride home she slept with her head on her dad's shoulder.

19

—·—

F rank sat in his pick-up truck, parked on the corner of
Roxbury Street, watching the entrance to 315
Grandview Avenue. He had rung the bell to apartment 5B; no
one was home. He had decided to sit out front and wait—for
what, he was not sure. He regarded any college-aged Black
male walking on the sidewalk with suspicious curiosity, but
did not see anyone who might fit the bill enter 315 Grandview.
Then after sitting there for over an hour he noticed a young
Black man with neatly-buzzed hair and a strong athletic build.
He wore an inside-out, gray sweatshirt carrying what looked
like a book bag over his shoulder. Jamal?

The young man stopped near the pathway that turned into
the project complex toward 315 Grandview and took out a
cellphone. He looked down and twiddled with both thumbs
and a couple of seconds later Frank heard the loud ding of a

message alert from Jen's phone, sitting in his console. It *was* him. The text message was still visible on the screen: *Where R U?*

A surge of adrenaline shot through Frank's veins. He had found him. But now what? He had not so much formulated a plan as he had let one event lead him to the next. Was he angry? At whom? Jamal—maybe. Jen—definitely. But why? Certainly she was old enough to date, he just hadn't really considered the fact that she might date someone who wasn't Irish or Italian. Was he upset that Jamal was Black? Of course not, he answered himself quickly. He wasn't a racist—his race had nothing to do with it. Frank knew the projects better than his naïve daughter, better than anyone! It wasn't just race. It wasn't just poverty. It was a different world—a world he didn't want his daughter to have any part of.

His hands were shaking. He had lost Diane. He had wasted time and taken her for granted. "I won't lose Jen," he said aloud. He reached under his shirt and pulled his shield up and left it hanging over the front of his shirt. He felt for his gun through his shirt and ensured it was still covered. He pulled the door handle up and pushed the door out with his leg. He still had no plan.

He was parked about a hundred feet away from Jamal, and as one foot hit the asphalt an elderly woman approached the young man. She too was Black, with white hair and a cane in her hand. She moved slowly and had her other hand strung through two shopping bags. When Jamal noticed her, the two exchanged a brief dialogue and he relieved the woman of the shopping bags. He then walked slowly next to her around the corner of his building, to an entrance at the back. Frank froze and then quickly got back in his truck.

Tears ran down his cheeks. He began sobbing now; his anger had drained. All that was left was grief—the grief he had bottled-up since Diane had died. Sure, he had cried at the hospital and at the funeral, but he had not wept. He now did so with abandon. He gripped the steering wheel tightly with both hands and cried loudly in the quietude of his pick-up. Children walking by looked in; Frank's sobs must've been audible through the windows. He didn't care. He rested his head on top of his hands on the steering wheel and repeated, "I miss her so much," over and over.

He cried hard for a full minute before catching his breath and wiping the tears from his cheek. A strong gust of wind bent the large tree standing on Grandview Avenue, thirty feet or so from the corner, opposite the entrance to Jamal's building. Frank watched as golden-brown leaves abandoned their swaying branches and rained down on the patch of spotted green grass that wrapped around the tall, red-bricked building.

He started the motor and drove away.

20

J en, Bridget, Halper, and two other C.S.I. students—a
young woman with red-framed eyeglasses and a New York
Yankees cap, and a guy who looked to be in his mid twenties
wearing a gray hooded sweatshirt with *College of Staten Island*
in large purple and black letters. The five sat facing each other
in a small clearing. Behind them was the domed bivouac tent
Halper had set up. They were huddled close in the cramped
space with other tents pressed up against their backs. Darkness
had fallen, but the chants and drumbeats persisted in the near
distance. The number of protestors had fallen while the
number of cops had increased. The five shared whatever food
they had: granola bars; bananas; chips and the like. There were
people among the crowd handing out sandwiches but Jen
wasn't hungry enough to try the unknown.

"You know what I haven't seen yet?" blurted Bridget amid giggles. "A drum! I mean... Where the hell is the drumbeat coming from?"

Halper laughed and half-choked on a granola bar. "Right there," he said, pointing over her shoulder and the two continued laughing at themselves.

Jen realized they were high. She guessed they had stopped somewhere on their way back from the rally at Police Headquarters. Her disdain for the professor deepened.

"I mean, who knows? Maybe it *will* grow. Maybe people *will*, like... wake up," said the young woman with the Yankees cap. "If people demand better regulations and a fairer system of taxes, maybe things *will* change."

"They'll never allow it to grow—you'll see," answered gray-sweatshirt guy, an unlit cigarette hanging out of his mouth. "Sooner or later the cops will storm this park and arrest everyone. They say *now* they'll allow a peaceful protest. So they'll invent another reason—like the Parks Department needs to get in here to rake the leaves or something—You'll see!"

"Fucking pigs!" belted Halper before bursting into a fit of snorting laughter.

"Shhh!" squeaked Bridget as she leaned over to cover Halper's mouth, though she too was laughing. "I told you she doesn't like that kind of talk."

"It's fine, Bridge. Don't change your conversation on my account," said Jen. She was losing patience with her friend.

"Hey, look," said Halper, "I don't know your old man—he could be the greatest guy in the world for all I know. I just mean that the police as a whole, by definition, do the bidding of the powerful. Corporations buy elections, politicians work for them—and the powers that be have the police to make sure no one fucks with their profits too much."

It seemed strange to Jen to hear her professor say fuck, but then again, the whole day was strange. "You think it was corporations my dad was worried about when he was being shot at in the ghetto?" she asked.

"No," he answered quickly, "but I do think the rich have an interest in keeping a lid on the poor communities. I think they're more interested in making sure there are plenty of cops to arrest drug dealers and turnstile jumpers than they are in making sure there are enough teachers in those neighborhoods."

"Yeah but if kids get shot on their way to school, what good are the teachers?" said the Yankee-capped student as she reached for a bag of chips. "Don't we need cops to keep the neighborhoods safe?"

Gray sweatshirt guy nodded his head in agreement.

"I'm here because I believe in this movement," added Jen. "I think that Wall Street's greed almost destroyed this country. I think the politicians let them off easy. I think we're here to say something that needs saying. But to me, the cops around the barrier are just working stiffs. They're not the enemy."

Halper began laughing uncontrollably. He was snorting loudly and holding his side. Bridget laughed loudly too, without seeming to know why.

"Talk about your daddy issues," said Halper between snorts.

Jen got up and walked away.

Halper was laughing as Bridget called out to Jen. When her friend was gone, Bridget turned back toward him. "That wasn't very nice," she said before she too let out a giggle.

"I'm just messing with her," he answered. The other two looked on silently. They weren't Halper's students.

"You know, her mom just died and she *is* having a tough time with her dad right now," said Bridget.

"That sucks," said the guy in the gray sweatshirt.

"And now she's dating a Black guy and she's afraid of what her dad is going to say," she added in a hushed voice.

Halper looked around for Jen but didn't see her. He tried to focus on what Bridget had just said, but his mind was cloudy and he was hungry. He bit into a granola bar and scanned the crowd while he chewed. Her mother had just died!

21

Frank sat on Leon's living room couch and polished off the last sip of beer in the bottle. Leon returned from the kitchen and handed him another. The green glass bottle had frost on the outside; Leon had put them in the freezer. Frank put the chilled rim to his lips and tilted his head back. The icy-cold beer swished past his teeth and numbed his cheeks and tongue as it slid down his throat. He gulped deeply three or four times and when he rested the bottle—still in his hand—on the armrest, it was half empty.

Leon sat back in the sofa. He looked to Frank and waited. Frank twirled the bottle in his hand and stared at the beer spinning round inside. He could feel Leon looking at him. Frank was quiet for a moment more, then said: "I don't know what I would've done last week without you and Bev. Jen really seems to open up to you two. I wish she'd open up to me."

"Give her time. Give her time. Where is she anyway? How did she make out with her school project?"

"What project?"

"At the museum—saw her this morning on the ferry. Said she was going to the museum."

Frank shook his head. "I don't know where she is. She left her phone at home. She sent a message from her friend's phone saying she was staying at her house tonight."

"She's a big girl. I'm sure she's fine. She just needs a little space."

"But I need her here," answered Frank softly. "I think I'm cracking up, Leon."

"What else is new!?" Leon said with a smile.

"She's got a boyfriend and today I went looking for him."

"And..." Leon responded.

"And... I saw him." Frank would not look up.

"Well..."

"He lives in the Mariners Harbor Projects."

"Hoooh! Don't tell me she dating a brother!"

Frank now looked Leon straight in the eye. "Do you think I'm a racist?"

Leon reached forward for his beer and took a long sip. He sat back again, holding the beer in his hand and resting it on his knee. "Why would I think that?"

Frank leaned forward and adjusted his butt-cheeks in the armchair. He took a quick sip of beer, as a batter taps his cleats and adjusts his batting gloves before stepping in the box— getting all the nervous prep-work done before focusing on the task. Ready now to speak he began slowly. "Diane and I always tried to show Jen a good example. We were careful with our language; we tried not to curse in front of her. And Diane especially was like a hawk with not letting anyone use racial slurs around her. We never wanted her to hear the kind of language we grew up hearing. We sent her to P.S. 45 instead of Catholic School in part because we wanted her to be around white *and* Black kids."

"Well clearly you succeeded," said Leon with a laugh. "So that's why you came here?"

Frank looked up, not getting the reference.

"You want me to tell you you're not a racist?"

Frank took another sip of beer, avoiding Leon's gaze.

"What happened when you found him? Did you talk to him?" asked Leon.

"No. I was going to, but I stopped. He helped an old lady with her grocery bags."

"He's a good kid?"

Frank nodded.

"Because he helped that old lady?"

Frank summoned the courage to look his old partner in the eye and again nodded.

"What if the old lady wasn't there?" Leon asked gravely.

"What do you mean?"

"Suppose the boy was just walking home—minding his own business and didn't see an old lady with groceries?"

Frank didn't respond and Leon continued: "Would a white kid have to prove himself by doing good deeds?"

Frank finished the beer and placed the bottle on the coffee table. He stood quickly, started to say something and then stopped. A moment later he mumbled: "Thanks for the beer," as he went out the front door.

Leon raised his voice and called after him: "I thought you came here to have a conversation."

22

—·—

Jen stood in front of the deli, underneath the awning, hoping the rain would soon stop. She sipped tea and stared at the tents and poncho-covered protestors across the street getting wet. She found the sound of rain soothing. It was crowded under the awning and two young men, teens really, were close enough for her to hear their conversation:

"Dude—you should've done it today. It would've been perfect—getting arrested in front of police headquarters."

"I didn't want to miss Radiohead."

"Dude—I told you that was bullshit. There's no way they'd show up here. There's no room and they're not allowed to use amps."

"I'll do it tomorrow."

"On the bridge?"

"Yeah it'll be sweet. I'll just push one of the cops."

"No dude—I told you. It *has* to be nonviolent. Just trespass somehow. Go behind a barricade and sit on the ground."

Jen turned to look at them. Young. White. She put her hood up and stepped out into the rain to cross the street.

23

—·—

J amal sat on a bench in the Grandview Avenue playground, across the street from his building. It was dark and though he'd felt a few drops earlier, it hadn't rained much in Mariners Harbor. There was a pick-up basketball game going on in the fenced-in court opposite the bench. The group was boisterous and yelled taunts at each other each time the rubbery ball ricocheted off the netless rim. He couldn't see the game—the small fenced-in city swimming pool blocked his view—but he could almost follow the action by the sound of sneakers scuffing on the painted-asphalt key and the sound of dribbling, followed by the silence of a tossed shot and the bouncy thud, unless the shot scored cleanly.

He stared down at the darkened screen of his cellphone and wondered why Jen wasn't answering his calls or texts. He had even texted that he was sorry, although he wasn't entirely sure he owed her an apology. Maybe he should've gone with her today. Why'd he have to be so stubborn? Then he thought of the funeral. He had told Jen it didn't bother him that she'd asked him not to come, but now it did. "I understand how you feel," Jamal whispered to himself. That's what Jen had said about him not wanting to go to Zuccotti Park. That's what bothered him now. How could Jen ask him to stay away from her father, keep out of sight, yet presume to understand how *he* feels—what *he* is thinking? She didn't know how it felt to be Black—to be looked at with suspicion for no other reason than her skin color. If she got locked-up, she could just call her dad who could probably fix it so that it never happened. What about him? Who'd fix it if he got locked up? Certainly not Jen's dad.

He tried to remember that Jen wasn't the enemy. She was different from other white girls he knew at school. She saw *him*—not some social experiment to be spoken to in overly politely tones as a façade of toleration. He liked her and now he wondered if he had overreacted. He knew she cared about him and this drained his anger, leaving only sadness—which was always harder. Sadness saps out self-confidence and leaves you feeling lost.

Jamal felt completely lost.

A young man approached.

"Ssup yo?"

Jamal looked up. The man was around the same age, slightly shorter and had a brand new Cincinnati Reds cap on—the brim totally flat, the sales tag dangling from the button on top, and a silver sticker on the face of the brim showing the cap size. He wore it with the brim off to one side.

"Ssup, Marcus!" returned Jamal with a head nod.

The young man sat and held out a bottle wrapped in a brown paper bag. Jamal looked at it for a second. He knew better than to drink alcohol outside. Such things were cop-magnets. He looked at the bottle and decided he didn't care. He grabbed it and took a long swig. It was sharp tasting and barely cold—probably malt liquor or a cheap beer. He didn't ask, just handed the bottle back.

"You seen Tina out here?"

Jamal shook his head, "Naa... Ain't seen her in weeks."

"Bitch is pregnant! Tsss... I know that shit ain't mine. She got some nerve laying that shit on me!" He took a sip from his bottle and offered another sip to Jamal.

Jamal drank again and gave it back. So close, he thought, no matter how hard he tried, he'd always be an inch away from this life. Get a girl pregnant. Get locked up. There it was—you were stuck here in the projects forever.

"You still at C.S.I.?"

"My second year," Jamal answered with slight embarrassment. It would have been easier to say he'd dropped out.

"You the smart one. I'm going to do the same... get my G.E.D., go to college—that's the smart thing to do."

Jamal nodded, knowing he would do none of those things.

A black sedan drove onto the sidewalk and blocked the entrance to the playground. The doors swung open quickly. The two young Black men knew exactly who it was. Jamal just sat still, with his hands in front of him, still holding his phone. Marcus tried to set the bagged-bottle down on the ground quickly but it was too late. He'd been spotted holding it.

The men who approached were both white and probably in their late twenties. One wore a football jersey and the boxy outline of his bulletproof vest could be seen underneath it. The other wore a fleece sweater and it was harder to make out the vest underneath. Both had badges hanging from chains around their neck and their right hands were on their still-holstered guns. One had a large, black metal flashlight shining on Marcus and Jamal and the other clutched a police radio.

"What's going on fellas?" asked the cop with the flashlight as he knocked the bottle over with his foot and saw the foamy liquid spill out. "Little partying in the park?"

The other cop now spoke, more sternly. "Stand up, both of you, and put your hands on the fence."

Both Jamal and Marcus complied. They had each been through this before. They knew the drill. The echoing, female voice of the police dispatcher squelched out of the radio and echoed off the benches and children's slide as the cop holding the radio put it closer to his ear. The other had his in his back pants-pocket.

"In the confines of the One-two-o, a Ten-fifty-three with injuries at the corner of Bay Steet and Vanderbilt Avenue. Calling O-Adam... O-Adam on the air..."

Neither cop paid any attention to the dispatcher's voice.

The cops patted them down and then told them both to sit.

"You got I.D.?" asked one of the cops.

Jamal pulled a wallet out of his back pocket and slid out his driver's license. The other young man pulled a white card out of his front pocket—no wallet. One cop took Jamal's license and the other grabbed the white card.

"Benefits card... There's a shock," said the one cop. He also took Jamal's license and walked a couple of feet away. He switched the channel on his police radio and held it to his mouth. "One-two-o-Crime-one to Central for a warrant check."

Jamal and Marcus sat again, the cop with the flashlight looking down on them. The radio in his pants pocket was still making noise.

"In the confines of the One-two-o, a Ten-ten, shots fired in the vicinity of Castleton Avenue and Broadway. Unit on the air..."

After a few minutes the other cop returned. He handed Jamal his driver's license and nodded to Marcus. "Ten-eighteen on this one," he said to his partner and they both put their hands on the seated man's shoulders—simultaneously standing and spinning him. In an instant he was handcuffed. Jamal knew better than to interfere—or even speak.

The cops took their prisoner to their car and put him in the back seat. Marcus had not even argued. The arrest didn't bother Jamal. Marcus had probably blown off a court appearance. He should have known better. Walking around with an open warrant is asking for trouble. Jamal watched the cops put Marcus in the back of the car and then open the two front doors. On the passenger side, closest to Jamal, the cop made eye contact with him as he stooped down clumsily to get his Kevlar-vested torso into the seat. The cop wasn't much older than Jamal. The two locked stares and Jamal blinked—turned his head. The car drove away.

Now Jamal was angry. Not because Marcus had been taken away, but because the cop had made him feel small. There was nothing Jamal could do. What Jamal never told anyone was that he wanted to be a cop to stop feeling powerless. He wanted the roles of that encounter reversed. He didn't want to be the kid watching his brother being taken away.

Why should that white cop have such power and not him? He could feel the way that cop looked at him and now he thought of something else: That is how Jen's dad will look at me. He picked up the bottle that had been kicked over. The brown paper bag was wet, but the bottle was still about a third full. He took a sip and swallowed it slowly, then placed the bottle upright on the ground under the bench.

24

F rank sat on a barstool intent on enjoying his beer without talking. The man on the stool next to him, however, had other ideas.

"He's got some power. Watch that—just punches it to the opposite field," said the man looking up at the television. A replay of a regular season Robinson Cano homerun was playing.

Frank watched Cano round the bases. "They've got a good chance—if they take tomorrow night too. Detroit'll never come back from two games to nothing," he responded, hoping the small talk would be brief.

"They need this kid to stay hot," the man added, pointing up as Cano crossed the plate. "He can't choke like he did against the Phillies two years ago." The man was in his sixties. Frank had seen him at the bar before but never got his name.

He was balding and the grayish hair on his temples was shorter than the hair growing out of his ears.

"The Yankees aren't what they used to be," Frank said. "Jeter is old. A-Rod's best days are behind him—and C.C. is their only reliable starter." The T.V. was now showing a tarp-covered infield as rain poured down on the empty ballpark. The volume was off, but the commentators must have agreed that Cano was the key to the Yankees' success. They were showing another clip of the second baseman's regular season highlights.

"They just don't respect the game like they used to," the man offered. "You think if Mantle... or Maris ever went three for twenty-two in the World Series they'd ask for more money next contract?"

"I didn't realize his contract was up?" said Frank. He finished his beer and put the coaster on top of the glass so the bartender wouldn't refill it.

"They're all the same," the man added. He then looked over his shoulder and did a visual sweep of the bar. "What do you expect?"

Frank knew exactly why the man surveyed the bar. He had seen that sweep many times: in the schoolyard; in the dugout; in the precinct locker room. Frank looked around the bar as well. Everyone was white.

25

The night was crisp and damp. The rain had let up but everything in the tightly-packed park was wet. The drumbeats and the chanting had stopped and most of the protesters were in their tents or cocooned in sleeping bags laid out on black garbage bags in the open. Someone was sleeping on every bench. It was difficult to walk without stepping on a tent or a snoring lump in zipped-up nylon. Jen had stayed up later than most listening to a lecture, but now weaved her way back to Halper's tent.

She found the professor sitting outside in front of the tent door-flap. He wasn't wearing his glasses and he had his fleece pullover on with no shirt underneath. The front zipper was low to reveal his hairy bare chest. His hair was disheveled and he was smoking a cigarette. Jen could see Bridget asleep in the tent. She was cuddled up in the sleeping bag with a bare shoulder protruding above the top. She knew her friend had just fucked her professor and the thought turned her stomach.

Jen was about to spin around and walk away when Halper spoke in a surprisingly kind tone.

"I'm sorry to hear about your mom."

Jen froze. "Thanks."

Halper tapped the bottom of the soft-pack and a lone cigarette slid up through the top. He offered it to her.

She shook her head.

"My dad died when I was seventeen," he said as he ripped a piece off the flattened cardboard box he was sitting on. He offered it to Jen.

"I'm sorry," she said, placing the cardboard on the wet ground and sitting.

"Hardest part's to come. Then it'll get better."

"What do you mean?" she asked.

He took a long drag and exhaled through his nostrils. "When did she die?"

"Little less than two weeks ago."

"People call a lot? Do they stop by—drop off food?" He asked dryly.

"Good amount. My aunt. My dad's partner and his wife. Yeah, last week, anyway. This week I went back to school and went out almost every night, so I don't know."

"You should have said something when you came back. Tell your other professors. Don't let them mark you absent for last week, you're excused," he said in a business-like manner as he puffed out more smoke. "It'll stop—the people coming by I mean. You'll see. Everyone will go back to their lives in a few weeks and that's when it gets hard. That's when you'll really start missing your mom."

He took another drag and continued, "It's the way it's got to be, really. I mean, what would the world be like if everyone grieved every loss they knew of? Could you imagine? Your second cousin dies and you become depressed for a year. No. Our grief is our own. It's one of the very few things in this world we own completely. Joy is shared, but grief—grief is private. Even if the people next to you have the same grief themselves, yours is your own."

"So what got you through it?" asked Jen. She zipped up her sweatshirt and pulled up the hood. A chill had set in her body.

"I found a new normal. After the weirdness between my mom and me and my sister, we found a way to get through the day. Eventually, it didn't feel weird anymore. It just felt normal."

"It feels real weird with my dad right now," she responded.

Halper nodded and took a last, long draw from his cigarette before smashing it out on the ground in front of his crossed knees. "Mom did all the talking, right? Now you don't know what to say to each other."

She smiled joylessly in acknowledgment.

"And you got a Black boyfriend to spring on him to boot."

Jen looked up quickly in embarrassment but before she could respond, he spoke again.

"Do you think it'll bother him?"

She shrugged her shoulders

"Does he not like Black people?"

She shook her head firmly. "His best friend is Black."

"So what's the problem?" he shot back quickly.

"I just... I just... I don't know how to say it. I definitely think he hates the projects. He used to work in the projects in Brooklyn and was in shootouts and stuff and I think he'd flip out if he knew Jamal lived in the projects." Jen didn't care that she had said his name: *Jamal!* If Hapler could screw a student, she could date a classmate. She didn't care that he knew. "Him and my mom weren't racists. But he's old-fashioned, my dad, and I feel like he'd always assumed I would marry a guy from the neighborhood or something. He never said anything, but... I can't explain it. I guess I'm just nervous to tell him about Jamal and that makes me feel guilty. I feel guilty that I'm nervous—like maybe that makes me a racist... being ashamed of him or something."

"Nah," Halper answered. "You're just nervous. It's like an old Band-aid, rip it off quickly. Just come home with Jamal at a time you know your dad is home and introduce him. That's better than having some awkward conversation. I'm sure it'll be fine. Jamal is a nice guy—your dad will like him."

Jen smiled.

Halper stood and shook his leg. "Cramp," he said as he massaged his right calf. He stood upright and looked at her. "This is going to be a tough year—because of your mom and all. Last thing you need is to have something that's got nothing to do with your mom come between you and your dad. Give your dad a chance." He turned toward the tent.

"Professor..."

He turned back.

"Thanks," she said with a little smile.

"No problem," he answered. "You got a sleeping bag?"

"Just a blanket, in my backpack."

"I'm going for a walk—not much of a sleeper. Why don't you sleep with Bridget in the tent? Sleeps two, and you'll be warm."

She wasn't sure about lying down next to Bridget, but she really didn't want to sleep out in the open on the hard ground with just a small blanket. "Thanks," she said again. "Can I ask you something?"

"Shoot."

"Are you worried?" She nodded toward the tent. "Someone could find out at the college."

Halper laughed. "Nah. I was thinking it was time to give C.S.I. a break anyway. Maybe I'll travel around Europe or something." He looked back toward the tent. "Maybe she'll come with me." He smiled almost sadly and after a moment added, "You never know."

He walked away and Jen entered the tent. Bridget slept peacefully, facing the other way. Jen took out her blanket and set herself up next to her friend, using the backpack as a pillow. She zipped the tent door shut and it was now completely dark as she lay back.

26

──·──

F rank sat alone in his living room unable to sleep. The T.V. was showing crime-drama reruns with the volume off. Colorful shadows danced silently across the darkened wall while Frank stared at the revolver on the end table beside the armchair. He picked it up and removed it from the holster, feeling the weight of it. The handle grip was hardened black rubber and he wrapped his hand around and slid his finger through the trigger guard. The hammer was enclosed inside the body of the gun to prevent accidental discharges. Frank ran his left index finger over the gun's brushed-silver metal. He opened, spun, and reclosed the cylinder—inspecting the five rounds inside. He held the weapon up in front of his face with the barrel pointed up as if to fire in the air.

Finality had always fascinated—and terrified—Frank. How one split-second could have such profound, and often horrible, repercussions for the rest of your life. A hiker walks along a trail thinking of his or her life, loved ones, career, all the memories and all the future plans, everything that makes that hiker alive. Then the hiker trips and falls down the steep side of a hill and dies. In that second it is all over. Guns were the ultimate expression of finality. Frank and Ray had been driving around Brownsville, talking and joking, like a thousand times before. Then Ray stepped out of the car and a bullet he never heard or saw took away everything from him in an instant. If he had gotten out of the car a millisecond slower the bullet may have missed and Ray would never even have known how close death had been.

That's all it would take—one pull of the trigger. All the pain and all the regret would vanish in an instant. Try as he did to love the people close to him, Frank couldn't see how he had ever done anything but hurt them. He never treated Diane the way she deserved. Jen hated him. And now he had disappointed Leon. Tears ran down his cheeks and his hands shook.

27

J en lay awake in the tent. She thought first of Jamal. She felt guilty for a second, thinking of him first so soon after her mom died, but she couldn't help it. She loved him, she thought—if this was indeed what love is. Things had ended weirdly the night before and she hadn't talked to him all day. It was probably a good thing. She needed to clear her head.

Now she thought of her mom. Her poor mom. She was a good woman—such a good woman—and she would miss out on so much. Jen thought about herself at that moment, in the middle of a crazy protest rally, sleeping in her professor's tent next to her naked friend. Could her mother see Jen? Could she see her right now? Here? Now?

She then thought of her dad. She couldn't remember the last time she told him that she loved him. Not since becoming a teenager, at least. She thought of how weird it would feel to say it now. She reached over Bridget and fished around the darkness for her phone. She found it. She knew Bridget's passcode and was about to open the home screen. Was it wrong to use her phone without asking? She just wanted to text, but what other texts would she see if she opened it? After a minute's deliberation, Jen put the phone back.

28

F rank held the gun to his head. He closed his eyes and thought about Jen. She'd be better off, he told himself. She'd be free. He cleared his mind and thought about the blackness before him. He steeled his nerves, tightened his grip, and gently pulled on the trigger. He felt the hammer move.

The loud, echoing, ding of a text message alert rang out from Jen's phone. Frank opened his eyes and relaxed the tension on his finger. He was disoriented. He lowered the gun and picked up the iPhone from the coffee table. Jamal again: *I need to see u.*

Frank looked down at the text. He wondered where the hell Jen could be. Another text came through: *u still @ ZP?*

What the hell was ZP? He thought for a moment and then it clicked. He looked at the gun in his hand and thought about Jen. She was at Zuccotti Park. She was surrounded by all the insanity he'd been seeing on the news. His eyes watered up and he placed the gun down on the table. She wouldn't have been freed, he told himself. She would have been sentenced.

29

Saturday

Jen woke achy in her knees and back and shoulders from the hard ground. She reached and unzipped the door flap just enough to see the overcast sky beginning to brighten. There was little activity in the park; most were still asleep. The noise of traffic was distant and faint—a horn here, a bus motor there. She sat up and looked toward Bridget, lying flat on her back with her bare arms bunching the sleeping bag to her chest. Bridget brushed her wild, hairspray-crusted red hair away from her eyes and looked up at Jen.

"Where is he?" she asked with a dry, cracking voice.

"Said he'd be up walking or something. He told me to sleep in here," answered Jen, making brief eye contact without holding a stare. "Hungry?"

Bridget nodded.

"Get dressed. We're going to the diner—my treat," said Jen as she nudged her friend's shoulder.

They gingerly hopscotched over sleeping bags and tents. There was no sign of Halper. They went out of the park and walked a couple blocks up Broadway and grabbed a booth at the greasy spoon on Nassau Street—one of the few left in Manhattan. The financial district on a Saturday morning was a veritable ghost town and they were the only customers. The cook came around the counter with two menus in one hand and two coffee cups in the other, along with two saucers wedged between his fingers. He was middle-aged and portly and wore a white chef's jacket with faded grease stains on the sleeves and chest. On his head was a red bandana. In one graceful motion he set each of them up with cup and menu and returned behind the counter without speaking.

He returned instantly with a coffee pot in each hand—one with a brown rim and the other orange.

"Café?" he asked politely.

Both Jen and Bridget slid their cups forward instantly and as neither said *Decaf,* the man filled both with regular. He returned to the counter and they each added milk and sugar.

Bridget looked up at Jen. Her hair was now tied back in a tight bun. "I feel stupid," she said softly.

"Don't," answered Jen quickly.

"I'm sorry for laughing yesterday. I didn't mean to—it was the pot, I swear."

"I know. It's fine."

"Do you think I'm a slut?" Bridget asked while stirring her coffee too forcefully.

"No. You're an adult. You did nothing wrong."

"You must think he's a sleazebag."

Jen shook her head. "At first I did. But now... Who knows? Maybe I was just being uptight. Life's too short to worry about bullshit. If he makes you happy, who cares! Just don't be naïve. He's older than you and I don't want to see you get hurt."

The cook returned and glanced from one to the other. "Señorita?"

"Toasted bagel with butter," said Bridget.

"Two eggs over, white toast, and bacon," said Jen.

The man scooped up both menus, went back behind the counter, and started making noise with eggs, whisks, knives, and dishes.

"I think it's over," Bridget said. "I thought he was sexy and I liked the attention he gave me, but I don't like the way I felt this morning—cheap."

"You're not cheap," answered Jen as she took a big swig of coffee. "You made a decision to start something and now you can make a decision to end it. It's your decision. You have the power."

Bridget smiled and sipped her coffee.

For a few moments they both stared down at their cups. Then Bridget spoke again. "So... How's it going with Jamal?"

Jen smiled bashfully and answered without looking up. "It's good," she said quietly.

She looked up and saw Bridget raising her eyebrows.

"We didn't speak yesterday. I mean—I forgot my phone and all but I could have called him from yours. It's just—there was a weird moment the other night."

"What do you mean?"

Jen shrugged her shoulders. "It's not important—he's a really nice guy. I feel bad."

"Is it the funeral? I think he would have liked to be there for you."

"I know. I wasn't thinking straight—I just couldn't deal with springing a new boyfriend on my dad right then." Jen paused, then added, "Not because he's Black."

"I know—I get it."

Jen wondered if Bridget was just being polite. Did that sound racist?

"I want to go home this morning," Bridget said.

"There's another march today—to the Brooklyn Bridge. I think I want to go," answered Jen. "I want to feel like I at least participated in something while I was here."

"Can't we just go home?" asked Bridget earnestly.

Jen took another sip of coffee and answered surely. "You should go. You had a long day yesterday and you're tired. I'll grab the first ferry after the march ends."

The cook slid thick, faded-white, oval diner dishes down on the table and the two ate hungrily and in silence.

When they emerged from the diner, Jen saw a very different scene from the one they had left. Broadway was teeming with news vans and gathering pockets of protestors. The number of police vehicles had doubled. She heard chants coming from the park but the drummer must have still been sleeping.

30

Finding parking on a Saturday along Richmond Terrace was never a problem and Frank pulled into a spot right near the terminal. He grabbed the three coffees in a take-out tray he had sitting on the passenger seat and walked down the long taxi ramp. The boat was about to leave and Frank was one of the last through the large sliding terminal doors before the worker shut them. The cops usually stood at the ramp watching all the passengers board, before turning to circle the passenger cabins after the boat shoved off. Frank and another man were the last onboard and the two cops had already started making their way toward the front of the boat.

He spotted Leon and his new partner Tim walking slowly past the sparsely-peopled benches. Frank trotted to catch up and tapped Leon's shoulder. He turned and looked at Frank.

A moment passed and Frank began to worry what he might say. Leon looked at the tray of coffees and the slightest of smiles turned up the corner of his mouth. "Cream, one sugar?"

Frank smiled and handed him a cup. "I got one for Tim too."

Leon took Tim's coffee and handed it to him. "You go on up ahead—I'll meet you on the forward deck," he told the young officer. Frank tossed the tray in a waste basket and opened the tab on the cup's cover. He took a sip and walked slowly next to Leon.

"I ever tell you about when I was sixteen?" Leon began, "I got my ass kicked by a couple of white cops."

Frank shook his head.

"Well it's true. After that I kept my ass clear of white cops. Cop walking the beat—I'd cross the street. Now here I am—a cop. I don't hold all white cops responsible for what those two did, even if that is my instinct—I resist it. You... You spend how many years seeing all kinds of fucked up shit in the projects and when you hear about this kid—that's the first thing that goes through your mind."

Frank remained silent.

"We can't help what pops into our mind," Leon continued. "All we can do is make our own decision based on our own values. We all got prejudices. What's important is that we *choose* to ignore them."

Frank nodded.

"Shit! I choose to be friends with you—you white-pig cop!"

Frank laughed.

"I remember when I first transferred to the Ferry Detail," Leon continued, "you were there a couple months before me, and that old man had the heart attack on the boat. You remember that?"

Frank nodded.

"You gave him mouth-to-mouth, kept him alive till we docked and E.M.S. showed up. He was Black and you worked on him like he was your own grandfather."

Frank shrugged his shoulders. "It's our job."

"We got to give aid. We don't got to give no one mouth-to-mouth. You went above and beyond and that ain't no little thing. Why you think I asked to be partnered with you after—What's his name?—McNeil got promoted?"

"I don't know, why did you?" asked Frank.

"Because I knew you'd always make the right choice. See I can take it if a white guy jumps to a conclusion about a Black guy if, in the end, he chooses to treat him fair. Figured, maybe you were prejudice, maybe you weren't. But if you can choose to give that old man the help—the dignity—he deserved, you couldn't be all bad."

"I grew up with a father that wouldn't let us play with the Puerto Rican kids in the Marlboro Houses," Frank said. "I didn't know any better."

"You *do* know better," Leon answered. "Give this kid a chance."

Frank smiled and held up an iPhone. "Jen's," he said. "She's at Zuccotti Park. He texted her this morning. He's on this boat."

31

J amal sat on a bench facing the rear of the ferryboat. He
had headphones stuck in his ears and a white chord hung
down across his chest to the phone he held in his hands. He
bobbed his head and silently mouthed lyrics. His eyes only
opened sporadically to glance down at the sneakers peeping
out of his baggy jeans. The heavy doors behind him, opening
onto the forward deck, swung in and back every minute or so
as passengers stepped out into the windy sea air and soon
returned to the calm of the cabin.

Jamal bobbed his head harder for a chorus and mid-refrain
opened his eyes to see a tall, mid-forties, white man standing
directly in front of him looking down over him. He was
startled and ripped the headphones out, leaving them to dangle
over his knee blasting music toward the floor.

"Jamal?" asked the man—sternly but not unkindly.

"Yeah," he answered tentatively.

"Frank Scala—Jen's dad."

Jamal could not have been more shocked if his own pants had suddenly burst into flames. "Oh..." he blurted. "Hey." He half stood and made to shake hands but Frank sat before he had the chance. Jamal sat back awkwardly.

"I'm going to find her," said Frank. "I assume you are too."

Jamal just nodded, still too surprised to speak.

"We can look for her together," said Frank before adding, "You go to school with Jen?"

"Yes Sir—C.S.I. We're in the same Poli-Sci class."

"What year are you?"

"I'm a sophomore."

"Major?"

"I didn't declare yet... I was thinking Poli-Sci."

"You want to go into politics?"

"Actually, I was thinking about law enforcement. I just signed up for the Police Department test."

Frank had clearly not expected that answer and nodded in muted surprise.

Jamal looked down at his feet to decide on his next sentence. "I'm sorry about your wife."

Frank again nodded, and then said, "Thank you." After a moment, he spoke again: "So, what did you two fight about the other night?"

An ice-water bucket of fear and embarrassment was dumped over Jamal. "Sir?" he asked feebly.

"Jen forgot her phone at home," Frank added.

Jamal felt a quick jolt of relief. She wasn't ignoring him.

"I saw your text—*Sorry about last night*—I figured you two had some sort of argument."

Jamal's head dropped. He was mortified and speechless.

"Was it because of me?"

Jamal was confused. "Sir?"

"I imagine that on some level Jen's been worried about what I might think about her having a..." he paused briefly and then added, "boyfriend. I hope that didn't cause the two of you to argue."

Jamal was dumbfounded. He had been nervous about meeting Jen's father and had sensed that Jen was nervous too. It had never occurred to him that Jen's father might care what they were feeling.

"No," Jamal began timidly, "We just, uh, had a disagreement. About something else."

Frank leaned back without speaking and Jamal considered waiting for a response but felt awkward with the silence.

"She wanted me to go with her to the protest."

Frank seemed surprised. "And you didn't want to?"

"I tried explaining to her. It's different for me. I get locked up and the police won't ever hire me. She asked me if I believe in Occupy Wall Street and I said yes—I meant it. But I can't get locked up."

"And that upset her?"

Jamal sensed Frank would be expecting an explanation, some kind of accounting for his reaction but he had nothing to give. In truth, had Jen simply gotten mad at him for not going with her he would have argued back and felt justified. It was her sympathy that had bothered him. *I understand how you feel*—she couldn't possibly, he thought. That's what had angered him the other night, but now he regretted his reaction. He had regretted it almost immediately but wasn't sure why, until now. Frank had just admitted being worried about their feelings. Maybe you didn't *always* have to be in someone else's shoes to empathize. He told none of this to Frank. He instead answered simply: "Said she understood."

"I see," answered Frank with a nod. "So why are you here now?"

"I don't like how we ended off the other night. I tried calling yesterday, but I guess she had no phone—so there it is."

Frank laughed dryly. "You were being sensible. She's her mother's daughter—stubborn."

Jamal thought it better not to comment.

The ferry was nearing the Whitehall Terminal at Manhattan's southern tip. Passengers were now gathering by the front doors. Two police officers waded through the crowd and Frank waved them over as he called out: "Leon!"

"This is Jamal," he said, turning his head toward the young man. "Jen's boyfriend."

Taken by surprise, Jamal cleared his throat and was about to speak but Leon beat him to it.

"You take care of that little sweetheart."

"I will, Sir."

Leon smiled and lightly punched Frank's shoulder.

"Jamal wants to be a cop," said Frank.

"You don't say!" Leon answered. "Well, we got time to talk him out of it. Stock brokers make more money."

Leon laughed heartily and Jamal looked to see Frank's reaction. He too was laughing.

32
—·—

J amal and Frank exited the ferry terminal and Bridget was
coming up the walkway from State Street. She had a duffle
bag slung tightly across her shoulders and was walking with
her head down.

"Bridget!" called Frank, seemingly startling her out of a
trance.

"Mr. Scala," she said with surprise in her voice.

"Where's Jen?"

Bridget looked at Jamal and then back at Frank and then
back at Jamal. "Is everything all right?"

"Yeah, everything's fine," said Frank in a calm voice.

Bridget was quiet for a moment but then must have realized
they were waiting for an answer. "There's a march over the
Brooklyn Bridge today. Jen wanted to go."

"You didn't?" asked Frank.

Bridget exhaled and answered in a slightly melancholic voice, "I'm tired."

Frank nodded his head.

"They at the bridge now?" asked Jamal.

"They were gathering—getting ready to march. There was a man standing on a bench—shouting directions and talking about economic justice and... um... passive resistance or something."

Frank let go of any anger he had felt the day before at Bridget for screening his calls and placed a hand on her shoulder. "Go get some rest," he said.

Bridget went quietly into the terminal.

Frank looked at his watch: 12:30.

"Next boat's one o'clock," he told Jamal. "Why don't you go find her? I'll wait here." Frank motioned to a bench alongside the terminal.

"Sir?" Jamal responded weakly.

"You go. You two don't need me making your conversation awkward. Go find her. Tell her what you got to tell her and then come back. I'll take the two of you out to lunch."

Jamal nodded and walked off..

Frank walked across State Street to a small newsstand. He knew it well; he had often hopped off the ferry to buy cigars here. The selection wasn't large, just a handful of brands that did well with passing commuters. He didn't know the names of the sizes: Robusto, Corona, Churchill. Those words were for the faux-afficionados, with their linen shirts and expensive watches—talking about cigars the way women talk about diamonds. Assholes. Frank measured cigars one way—time. He picked up one about the length of his index finger. Half-hour, he thought and brought it to the counter. The middle-easterner behind the counter recognized Frank immediately and took great pleasure in finally seeing him out of uniform.

"Hello, my friend. No work today?" he said boisterously.

"No work today," repeated Frank, with a forced smile.

Frank sat back on a bench in the small park between the ferry terminal and State Street. There were still plywood construction fences littering the park as the interminable reconstruction of the Ferry terminal dragged on. All was quiet today, however. There were not many people coming in or out of the terminal and the gloomy sky hung low over the desolate hub. Frank took the plastic wrapper off the cigar and smelled the brown leaf-wrap of the cigar itself. It smelled like humid cedar and autumn rain. It was firm, yet yielding to his fingers' squeeze and he thought of the man who'd rolled it, somewhere in the Dominican Republic—one of a hundred cigars he had rolled that day. Each cigar a handcrafted work of perfection—uniform yet unique.

Frank remembered his first cigar. He was a rookie in the Seven-three, one of the few nights as a rookie he was not on a foot-post. A veteran cop was out sick and Frank ended up in a car for the night with his partner. They each ate a slice of pizza from Pitkin Avenue while driving around from job to job, that way they could spend their meal period in peace. When their meal period came at 21:00, the old timer drove to an abandoned lot on Van Sinderen Avenue. It was desolate, tucked away under an elevated train track.

The veteran cop backed the car in, got out and pissed on a fence and then got back in the car. He shut the headlights and motor off and lowered the volume on his police radio.

"Never sit in a restaurant on your meal," he told Frank, "someone's always going to have some problem or question you'll have to deal with. And don't go back to the stationhouse either... Lieutenant's bound to find something shitty to stick you on. Eat on *their* time, while you're driving around, and then go somewhere and hide for your meal. It's the only peace you're going to get."

The old-timer had two cigars in his shirt pocket and he offered one to Frank. After some prodding, Frank took it and lit it with the match the veteran held out lit. He remembered the quiet that overtook the tiny corner of that crazy neighborhood. All the distant sirens and bottlebreaking and gunshots and shouts reduced to nothing. The far-off rumble of an elevated train and the September breeze were the only sounds as he held the velvety smoke in his mouth and exhaled slowly. His head tingled slightly and he felt his blood flow slower.

He now sat on the bench in front of the ferry terminal and bit off a small piece of the cigar butt and spit it at his feet. He opened the matchbook and flicked two sticks uselessly into the breeze before spinning and cupping his hands and finally getting one to light. Careful, he thought as he held the bluish-yellow flame to the tip of his cigar and puffed inward repeatedly to nurture it to life.

Nurture, he thought. That was the best word for lighting a cigar, which had, after all, a lifespan. It must be protected in its infancy with constant attention, constant relights and persistent puffing, before moving into the adolescent phase of that first good draw. The smoke pulled effortlessly now into your mouth with the ash on the end of the cigar lengthening like a teen boy's first stubble.

Frank held the first long draw a few seconds before pushing it out between his pursed lips. He heard the loud air-horn blast of the 12:30 ferry sounding out. He looked at his watch: almost *12:40*—ten minutes late. He thought about how many ferry trips he must have taken. He always checked his watch when the air-horn sounded. He took another long drag as the proud stogie fully matured into adulthood. It practically burned itself now, no need to relight, no heavy puffing to keep the red glowing. The ash tip held on for nearly three-quarters of an inch—the sign of a tightly wrapped cigar. Finally he relented and flicked the gray ash-head to the ground.

A woman walked swiftly up the walkway to State Street and she reminded Frank of Diane, though she looked nothing like her. He thought of her life. She had been nurtured and she had matured, only to be snuffed out in her prime. He wished he had done more for her. They'd had good times, but he wished he'd done more to make everyday a good time, to make her smile, to make her laugh. He thought of the last argument they'd had and regretted it deeply and helplessly.

The minutes ticked away on his watch and the cigar burned away peacefully, more than halfway gone now. Frank looked down at the now pyramid shaped ash-head slightly covering the red glow. He took in the earthy aroma of the rising smoke and appreciated the serenity it brought. Too often cigars are puffed through thoughtlessly until there is but a nub of it left; and only then is its owner keenly aware that the best part has burnt away, and puff as he might at the remnant—he will only get a bitter version of the once-sweet flavor that had sprung forth so effortlessly. The bitter flavor of wasted youth.

It was now 1:00 and Frank didn't see Jamal or Jen. Another ferry had docked and the people were now exiting the terminal, passing Frank on the bench and crowding the sidewalk along State Street. He crushed out the cigar, crossed State and headed up Broadway.

33

---·---

Jen was shoulder to shoulder with the slow-moving crowd as they inched closer to the Brooklyn Bridge entrance ramp. The sky was gray and gloomy above yet somehow held its rain. To Jen's sensitivity, the mood of the protestors was a sharp downturn from that of the smiling, chanting kids on their parents' shoulders the day before. She saw no children, just adults yelling and waving placards violently with the loss of innocence that adulthood brings. She cinched her backpack straps tight and kept her hands at chest level to keep from being pushed into the person in front of her.

As the crowd crossed the street circling City Hall Park and approached the promenade that leads to the bridge, Jen could see a waist-high, wrought iron fence dividing the approach. The crowd moved slowly, as a single body, and Jen was corralled to the right of the fence. As she moved further up the ramp, she realized that the pedestrian walkway had been to the left of the fence and she was now on the roadway of the bridge. There was no danger of cars, however, as traffic was completely blocked by the marchers. Even the cops, who had been at the front of the march trying to keep order, seemed to be backing up the roadway as well—perhaps directing the protesters away from the too-crowded walkway.

Being shorter that most of the men surrounding her, Jen felt enveloped by chaos. She heard chants and cowbells and drumbeats and police whistles all melting into one constant and therefore unheeded noise, like a ringing of the ears. Only the Brooklyn Bridge's tall Gothic tower arch stood above the mass of bodies in front of her. She approached the iconic stone archway as a pilgrim moving slowly toward a distant cathedral, its point in the sky her only reference of distance.

F rank found Jamal at a barrier in front of Zuccotti Park.

"I searched the whole park. She ain't here. Last of the marchers just went off to the bridge. She must be there," announced Jamal as Frank approached.

"Let's go," Frank answered and motioned for Jamal to follow. They took Broadway up to Park Row where they joined the tail end of the snaking mass of humanity slinking itself up the bridge's ramp. By the time they crossed from City Hall Park to the entrance promenade the police had blocked off the roadway to further marchers. Frank and Jamal instead went left at the wrought iron fence and followed the pedestrian walkway. The crowd was thinner at the rear and the two were able to cut around people as they moved forward in search of Jen. After a few hundred feet the line of people became a logjam and all Frank could do was step closer to the railing and look down at the roadway, now twenty feet or so lower than the pedestrian path. He pulled Jamal to the side with him.

"We'll never find her here," said Frank. "It's like a needle in a haystack."

The massive support cable that smoothly curved up toward the stone tower hung just a few feet over Frank's head. He laid his hands on the rusted, paint-peeled, horizontal truss that served as the railing and leaned his head out over the roadway. There were hundreds of protestors down on the roadway. How many? He couldn't tell. Five hundred, a thousand. Who knew? On the roadway also, at the head of the column were dozens of police officers. A line of blue-shirts held an orange, plastic mesh barrier straight across the roadway so the marchers could go no further. In front of the barrier were at least two dozen white-shirts—higher ranking officers. The protesters closest to the front were now seated on the asphalt with their arms linked. Then hundreds more stood, waving placards and yelling. He saw at least two people throw something forward —perhaps empty plastic bottles or something. Behind the mass of marchers on the roadway was a space of a hundred feet or so and then another line of police officers. The marchers were penned in.

Frank was shoved forward by passing marchers and Jamal put a hand on his shoulder to keep him from going over the railing. Where as before each small group was shouting their own chant, all the marchers on the pedestrian way now seemed to sing one common chorus:

"*Hey Hey.*"

"*Ho Ho.*"

"*Corporate greed has got to go!*"

Frank leaned across the truss to see the lower level. There was a commotion at the front of the crowd as small teams of cops seemed to pull up, handcuff, and drag off toward the orange barrier, various seated protesters. Frank could not see why those particular protesters were being arrested, but the bands of cops were only targeting certain people. One heavy-set, white-shirted cop leaned over to cuff a squatting woman and someone in the crowd grabbed his hat and threw it thirty feet forward into the hands of a cop at the barrier.

The march across the pedestrian way was now at a complete standstill. People began to climb up on the truss, holding on to the vertical cables that attached the main cables to the roadbed. Some even ventured onto the I-beams that crossed over the roadway.

On the roadway, the police began cuffing more and more people, pulling them to their feet and dragging them to the orange barrier.

"Why they arresting them?" asked Jamal, shouting to be heard.

Frank looked down over the scene and after a moment he figured it out. "They're arresting them for blocking traffic," Frank shouted back as he leaned toward Jamal's ear. "Look. See how they're only targeting the people sitting down right now. They figure those sitting are intentionally blocking the road."

"But they can't go nowhere," shouted Jamal.

"Mark my words..." Frank answered with a cracked voice. "Everyone on that roadway will be arrested!"

"It's like a thousand people down there!"

Frank didn't respond. He just scanned the crowd below.

Along the truss railing and up in the cables above, dozens of people held out smartphones, recording the chaotic scene below. Numerous taunts were yelled at the police from above and soon a new chant began:

"*The whole world is watching... The whole world is watching... The whole world is watching!*"

"Do you see her?" shouted Frank. He was having trouble distinguishing faces in the crowd.

"Look!" shouted Jamal, pointing to the rear of the pack. Standing with her gray sweatshirt hood up over her head was Jen. She was clutching her backpack straps with each hand. "Can we get her out of there?"

"We're sure as hell going to try," Frank answered as he pulled Jamal's arm back down the pathway.

By this point all of the protestors who were coming onto the bridge were on the bridge. The police had the roadway completely blocked off and isolated, beginning a few hundred feet up the ramp. Frank and Jamal made their way up behind the barricades. A line of cops stood facing the penned-in mass of protestors mid-span and two police vans were parked haphazardly in the road behind them.

Frank reached beneath his shirt and pulled up the chain with his dupe attached. He let it hang conspicuously over his light coat. As they approached the line, Frank approached the last cop on his right, a young looking patrolman resting his hands on his gun-belt. Frank tapped his shoulder and then walked between him and the cop to his left. Both noticed the badge and Frank nodded silently as he slipped through the line.

They approached the protestors and Frank turned to survey the line of cops—considerably more imposing from this vantage point. He wondered how the hell he'd get Jen and Jamal out and was then struck with a pang of regret. He should have told Jamal to wait back at the foot of the ramp by Park Row. It was too risky to bring him back there now. Jamal wasn't displaying a shield. They wouldn't just let him walk out. What the hell was he going to do?

They waded their way through the shouting crowd, some of the marchers now directing their taunts at Frank and his badge. They reached Jen and Frank tapped her shoulder.

Jen turned, looked at Frank and then Jamal. Frank saw terror in her eyes.

"Wha... What's wrong?" she blurted feebly.

Frank laughed and put both hands on her shoulders. "Nothing, sweetheart... Absolutely nothing."

"So you... You..."

"I just decided to take a nice ferry ride with my new friend here," Frank answered, almost shouting to be heard.

Jen gave a small laugh, but still seemed confused. Her eyes were teary. Frank was about to speak but Jen pointed at something back behind the line of cops. From the bottom of the roadway ramp, a city bus was backing up toward them. Frank saw two police officers walking slowly backwards and waving to the bus driver who watched them in his mirror. Down on Park Row, he could see two more city buses parked and waiting.

"What're they doing?" asked Jen.

Frank knew the answer but looked at Jamal without saying it aloud.

Jamal seemed to read Frank's mind and shrugged his shoulders in resignation.

"What is it?" yelled Jen.

Frank stood up on his toes to survey the situation as best he could. He turned back toward Jen to see her and Jamal standing close together and holding hands.

"They're getting ready to arrest everyone on the bridge!" he announced.

Jen looked up at Jamal and pressed her palm on his cheek. "I'm so sorry," she said.

"I'm the one who's sorry," he answered. "I should've been here with you from the start."

"Daddy," she said desperately, "Can you get us out of here?"

Frank looked back again and saw the line of cops now hunched around a group of white-shirts, getting their orders. "I think so, but not together. I'll have to make two trips."

The crowd of people tightened as screaming protesters at the back pushed forward. Some started sitting and locking arms. "Here they come," someone yelled.

"Take Jamal, Daddy, please. He can't get locked up—they won't let him be a cop."

Jamal began to speak and Frank cut him off. "She's right." Whether out of a sense of guilt for having initially distrusted the young man, or from sensitivity to his daughter's plea, he put aside his fatherly instinct and thought up a plan to get Jamal out first. He looked at the small bands of cops now twisting protestors' arms and cinching plastic zip-tie handcuffs around their wrists and made a decision. He put a hand on Jamal's shoulder and spun him around quickly.

"Give me your hands," he said as he pushed Jamal toward the police-line in the rear.

Jamal put his hands behind his back and Frank gripped his two thumbs tightly in one hand, keeping the other hand on his shoulder. To all outward appearances, he had him handcuffed. Frank looked to Jen. "I'll be right back, sweetheart," he said, just loud enough to be heard by her.

Frank leaned forward and spoke in Jamal's ear, "Struggle, but not enough to make it seem like I need help." He then winked, discretely, at Jen and shoved Jamal forward hard, dividing a pair of shouting protesters ahead of them. "Let's go, asshole," he barked loudly as he continued pushing his prisoner through the crowd. The shouting marchers surrounding them now noticed what was happening and they turned their anger on Frank.

"Fucking Pig!" yelled a young white woman with dreadlocked hair.

"Another Black man in jail!" yelled someone else.

Frank quickly moved through the pack as people moved aside both to see what was happening and to yell insults.

"Let me go, man, I didn't do nothing!" Jamal yelled as he twisted his shoulders, being careful not to pull his thumbs out of Frank's grip.

Frank ignored the insults and Jamal's pleas. He had plenty of experience with both. They kept moving. A few phones were held up above heads, recording the arrest. He pushed his prisoner between the sitting protestors at the crowd's edge and kept moving, even picking up his pace to assure the other officers he had it under control.

"Keep moving, asshole," said Frank loudly as he approached the cops who remained lined up across the roadway and a few made room for Frank and his prisoner to get through. He shoved Jamal down the ramp to the parked police vans and brought him around behind them.

"Where's your wallet?" Frank asked as he looked over his shoulder to see if anyone was watching.

"Back pocket."

"Keep your hands locked behind your back," he said as he took out Jamal's wallet and open it. He took a step back and pretended to be reading the driver's license. He casually looked around to see if anyone followed and waited a minute before putting the wallet back in Jamal's pocket. All attention seemed to be on the crowd on the bridge. Even the cops who had guided the bus up the ramp were back at the line.

"Don't run. Walk casually across Park Row and then get to the ferry terminal. We'll meet you there."

Jamal looked up into Frank's eyes. "Thank you," he said and walked off down the ramp.

Frank ran back toward the crowd but was stopped by a white-shirt—an angry Deputy Inspector whose salt and pepper mustache waved when he yelled. Frank's heart dropped, convinced the commander had seen him release a prisoner.

"No more plain-clothes officers. We're starting to lose control and I only want cops I can keep track of in there." spat the Deputy Inspector, not releasing his grip on Frank's arm.

"You got it boss!" Frank answered and back-peddled a few feet. The Deputy Inspector then went forward to yell at another cop and Frank walked toward the side of the roadway. None of the other cops was paying any attention to him. He took his badge and tucked it back under his shirt and ran forward into the crowd, not sure if he heard anyone yelling at him to stop. He snaked his way around the outside along the outer guardrail of the roadway, dodging two parked cars that had been abandoned mid-span by the drivers once the march overtook them. When he reached the spot where he thought Jen might be, he pushed people aside and wiggled his way through the crowd. The packs of police officers were now far into the crowd and they were handcuffing almost everyone they could get their hands on, one at a time.

As he approached Jen he called out to her. Before she could answer, she was spun around by two cops and had her hands cuffed behind her back in an instant.

"Jen... Jen!" he yelled and got within a couple of feet of her.

"Let her go!" he yelled at the cop who was finishing fastening the zip-tie behind her.

He put a hand on Jen's shoulder and pulled her toward himself, as if to stop the cop from finishing his work. "Let her go!" he yelled again, as the crowd swayed and cried out in one chaotic mass. "Let her go... I'm on the jo..."

"Shut the fuck up!" shouted a cop from behind, who had one of Frank's hands in his grip. Another cop seemed to come out of nowhere and had the other hand.

"I'm on..." Frank began before being shouted over by a woman who grabbed at the cop's arm. Frank tried twisting to free his arms but in seconds the plastic was zipped tightly around his wrists. The cops released their grip and Frank turned to speak to them but they had quickly moved ahead to cuff others. He let them go. He needed to find Jen. She was a few feet behind him, with other handcuffed protestors between.

Frank pushed toward her—hands behind his back. He shouted at people to let him through and finally was face to face with his daughter.

"Jamal's okay," he yelled as he leaned forward to try to get their faces as close as possible. The chants, the whistles, the screams all seemed louder now as the handcuffed waited—all now caught in their own personal protest. Jen was crying. He stepped forward and she leaned into his chest, rested her head on his shoulder and sobbed.

He wanted so badly to wrap his arms around her—to hold her tight like he did when she was a child. He put his mouth right up to her ear and said: "It'll all be fine, sweetheart. You'll see."

Jen picked her head up and looked at him. She was still crying. She looked so much like Diane when she cried. His heart broke for all the times he had failed them.

"Everything will be better now," he said as tears ran down his cheeks. "You'll see."

"Oh Daddy!" she said between sobs. "I love you! I love you so much."

Acknowledgments

I first began working on *Zuccotti Park* back in 2013. I had just published *The Dead Florentines* and was in the middle of researching for what would become *La Petite Parisienne*. I thought it would be fun (and easier) to write something brief about events more current than the Italian Renaissance or the French Revolution. I tried to keep the story simple. Though the Occupy Wall Street protests provided the backdrop, the true drama would center around the personal lives of a small group of ordinary New Yorkers. I soon discovered that simplicity is an art and if done well can be more difficult to achieve than complexity.

I was fortunate at that time to have a retired English professor to lean on. Judy Kirkpatrick was kind enough to read the manuscript and her notes reflected a lifelong passion for writing and an encyclopedic knowledge of literature. Her advice proved invaluable when I revisited the manuscript some seven years later.

I would like to thank my editor, Amber Hatch. I benefitted greatly from her enthusiasm and expertise. My children, Sofia and Luca—who are always so excited to hear that Daddy is working on a new book—inspired me. And finally, I want to thank my wife, Teresa for all the love and support she has given me since the day we first met.

A.S.

CPSIA information can be obtained
at www.ICGtesting.com
Printed in the USA
BVHW072255200222
629616BV00016B/584/J

9 781732 238046